CANDID ABOUT SPACE

S.E. SMYTH

To found and given moms: whatever forms, blood type, nurturing style, or relation.

CHAPTER 1

The door creaked open, and then it dropped hard on itself, and the sound resonated. Robert jumped back. "I thought it was my ex, Samantha. I thought she had barged through that door…My god." He held his hand to his chest. "Samantha wears that red sweater most days."

In the restaurant, bold light carried through small windows, casting shadows into the other room. This room bled darkness. Every minute was slightly different. In pleasing dips, Pauline pulled dark liquid from the edge of a small teacup, posing as a coffee mug. Residual brown lace decorated the inside of the mug just above the liquid's tempered fill. Half, Pauline noticed, remained. Pauline came there to talk.

"I, I wondered with as much as you do, do you ever get to pause? Everyone must get a break. The restaurant gigs…I can use that term." Pauline let out a declarative laugh.

She tried to lift spirits, lift the friendship. "It's, it's so brutal. Office work is much more savory. Less drama." She wanted to talk about everyday things, not recent events. Pauline looked down at her cup and thought the best of her cry for satiation, for caffeine. This antidote for laziness was not exactly what she wanted. Perhaps an espresso would've suited her.

"Come sit. I cherish the moments we get together. Being around each other is important," Pauline said.

Robert pulled his chef's hat off-kilter and then dropped it to his waist, caught in his hand so loosely it almost dropped altogether to the floor. A chef with a law degree, he would forever be a failure. His body collapsed into the cushioned chair perpendicular to the small two seat table that is barely a paid spot at the fine establishment. The space measured as much as a fleck of dust among the baroque, a cheaper, but

still reserved dot, among the embellishments, details, mold-
ings and furniture; and indulgences in art and character. The
staff arranged the centerpieces around the corner. The squir-
reled away spot is lonely in a corner, not intended for patron
use, where the manager does his bills and works with
receipts.

"I might go on about how she treated me or the ways she
didn't. Really, it wasn't worth our time. When she became
open about it, her need to see someone else. Ha. A woman
no less, I couldn't do anything else but understand." Robert
stood. Pauline understood his cached story. The things he
wanted to tell that rested on the tip of his tongue didn't come
out. Pauline watched him speak and then catch himself, then
he spoke again. "It's just…it's over." He lifted a weary hand
opposite the limp flange, holding a hat to look at the grit
under his fingernails. The grease that never seemed to go
away. "It's over. That much should be clear."

"She. It's not. She's sorry. It's…" Her friend sent Pauline
to talk, but the exact words wouldn't form.

The door slammed again, but Robert did not jump a
second time. When Monica entered, the room's staleness
escaped. Everything had dropped with the temperature outside. Robert wouldn't return. He wouldn't ask questions. She
came there to say specific things, to give him the dirty deal. He
said it himself. He comprehended the chain of events, what
had happened, anybody would. The mission to talk faltered.

Pauline lifted her hand and waved it loosely in the air,
almost an elbow, elbow, wrist, wrist, wrist shimmying down
her arm. Pauline had money, that much proved true, but
didn't act like a princess except in a loose sense of the word.
She directed from a back corner, telling Robert he would
have to make eye contact with someone else at the dinner
party tonight. He would have to move on because his ex had
moved on with a woman. Turn a sentry at his post and
march, slowly and intentionally, the other way.

Pauline sat in a dark corner next to the kitchen with a
single dim light. The delicate, inexpensive lamp cheapened

the spot, despite the fine silverware. The centerpieces in the well-lit section of the other room projected much more. A single bulb hid behind a tightly woven burlap shade, well-trimmed and sturdy in its structuring with a golden candle holder base with a loop for the finger. The fake gold made the thing seem like a farce of a fixture in this expensive place.

Her date with Monica would start in mere minutes, and she waited impatiently. Her foot tapped incessantly, and she avoided eye contact with every inanimate thing she laid eyes upon. Robert's anger, which pervaded, didn't die down. Monica would bring a lighter mood. She would talk about her daughter, their daughters, and the vacation they were all going on. Pauline relaxed and her spirits rose. They would all be a big, happy family. The dirty work done, now on to the next task. The trip would come in mere days.

"Monica. It's genuinely nice to see you. The girls, you see, are so eager to get going. I haven't even packed yet."

"This place is so fancy. Pauline, I can't."

"Oh, it's a small corner. No worries. I had to meet with a friend, Robert. He's so great. I mean. He's really a bang-up guy." She smiled weakly. She didn't want to elaborate anymore, even though Monica looked at her questioningly, begging for more, as expected in this place. "We'll get a real treat. This place is so expensive. But Robert invited me for dessert. They have a special new cake that's worth a try. And Robert is bringing out more coffee, or at least that he promised he would. It's my treat if it's not Robert's. I…a minute ago…dealt him some unwelcome news."

"Oh, my, Oh Jesus lord. I hope no one's died."

"Barely. Someone is now living their life. Making the most of it." She held herself back a bit, but then said, "Without Robert."

"Oh, I'm so sorry for Robert." She smiled meekly.

"Robert is an old friend. He'll get by. He can take care of himself. He's only a dog that doesn't get it when things are over. Aren't they all?" Pauline paused and leered. "Oh my, he truly is a good friend."

She leaned in to say these things, sharing a secret. They would have to gossip, that's what women did. Robert should know this, but she didn't want him to hear any more, so she marked it done. She wouldn't breathe another word. A remarkable woman placed herself in front of Pauline. Her daughter had paired them together. She wanted to ask Monica questions and smile about common things with her, not mumble about a man, no less one in the same room.

Monica did her the favor and changed the topic, leaning back and gushing, showing off her appreciation and wonderment, her openness to bond.

"Oh, Pauline. This is absolutely so wonderful. I'm so glad we get along. It's truly more than anything that we get along." She rubbed her index finger against the handsewn napkins, detailed in hand stitched blue and yellow flowers. "And this place is so fancy." She bit her lip as Pauline stared evenly and calmly. "We really should've told our daughters."

"Girls, shmirls. We're getting to know each other. It's that simple." Pauline lifted herself with her spine, arching her back and stretching a bit. "Hi. I'm Pauline. I'm divorced, single and mingling. Not with Robert right now, but I'm still looking for someone to spend those later years with. She looked down at her rich coffee. I'm retired and happy to go along for any ride, whether with my lesbian daughter and her girlfriend or a total stranger."

"Don't go hitchhiking now, Pauline." Monica waved her hand in Pauline's general direction, pushing her head to the side as she did it. "You are certainly too well off to go hitch-hiking or get abducted by a stranger, at the very least. Oh, did you mean me?"

"Oh, absolutely not," Pauline said. She gushed. "You are family. We are together forever if the girls get married. We might as well share their secrets with each other now." Pauline tapped the back of Monica's hand.

The kitchen helper refilled their coffee, and this time they sipped at the precious teacups sparingly. After the young man returned, begrudgingly bringing out the cake, and mumbling something about broken plates all the while, the pair of women, as if old friends, dug into the generous slices. Dense like lead and cut in a perfect triangle, the cake filled a full quarter, exactly, of the plate. The cake beckoned knife to mouth. Pauline imagined the processes Robert had gone through methodically, precisely, to prepare the cake. It weighed as much as a brick of gold. Chocolate wisps like eggshells crowded the top of the white mass. The icing lapped almost like stucco with sweeping indents in indents, perfectly scarred into the cladding with even strokes of a specialty knife. A cherry drizzle fell in a more happenstance manner, pooling in a small spot in the plate's corner. A full maraschino cherry topped the pool. "May I present Murder #1 from our new line of designer cakes?" The bus boy's voice had rung out, shivering under the scrutiny and pressure of two women, giving their full attention.

"Designer cakes. Oh God. That's how he's selling them. Look, this pool of cherry sauce is coagulating on the plate, something only to be served fresh. At least that's what I imagine." Pauline took a sadistic jab at the mass and then took a bite.

"It's something like designer drugs, you know it? Truly addictive. They should outlaw this cake." Monica nervously quipped about something her daughter or a friend had talked about way back when. She then stated openly that she, herself, had never done drugs, but she had friends who had partaken. She got it. Such things existed. And she expressed that this ornate restaurant and the delicacy cake, indeed, were like a drug.

Monica would likely steal away with this money, currency, power if she had the chance. She was here with Pauline. Pauline had inhibited it.

This whole affair became a special treat, a chef's restaurant dining experience. An important mark on the food map, an eater's map. This place would become something better, and the candle lamp would disappear. She imagined the whole place packed wall to wall, reservation only six nights a week. On Sunday, the chef would need the kitchen to experiment. They would have a first glance at what would be something. She presented herself this way. Whether or not true, she let on that the place surpassed her means. Pauline sounded grateful and a little jealous Robert didn't ask her to be his date the same evening, now that his ex, the one who was gone for good, would not be attending with him. She'd be there.

Robert's face had burned red, taking in the seconds, and broiling them, but Pauline would make up with him. She would find his courage and help him get back on his feet. He wanted nothing to do with her at the moment, but she would be there for him when he got himself ready. Pauline had been friends with Robert first, up and through his last attempt to send flowers and a cake. His very last effort was to resolve their issues.

As Samantha relayed, he had dropped by late at night one night, hoping to swoon her back into his arms. It backfired. She only called the police when he tried to open the new dead bolt. His attempts were innocent but brutally overstated.

He had a way of not understanding, not that he demanded anything from Samantha, that she must take him back, but pure innocence. He quietly mumbled to himself, "Why wouldn't anyone take me back?" To be fair, no one had told him outright, yelled into his ear, that he couldn't do what he did. That the relationship had ended some time ago.

Before that, he had daily lunches sent to her place at work. The front desk, under Samantha's direction, eventually denied the attempts to deliver. Robert showed up himself and reception told him to leave. When he came back, the staff lost all understanding. A big to-do happened one day when the secretary asked him to wait while she ruffled through policies looking for memos or loose verbiage in emails about ex's showing up at work. Robert left the office and didn't return.

The fact of the matter, the endless texts, the pining that Robert only saw as innocent complicated their relationship exponentially. Movies and romantic catch phrases, and words of advice from friends misled him. Pauline's assignment included being the only one to tell him the relationship had ended years ago.

Pauline took large chunks, placed her fork down, and chewed intensely. Monica took the smallest bits, tasting icing and cake separately, then together. She bent over the sculpture almost as if she needed glasses, examining the crumbs and the texture. She asked several times if they were in fact supposed to eat it.

When she finished with the cake, Monica wouldn't stop gushing. She over-thanked and asked if the chef would give her a moment of his time. Until that is, Pauline reminded her that Robert, a second ago, had gotten some unwelcome news.

"I'm sorry I must've interrupted," Monica said.

"Oh no, anything but. An excuse to lessen the brunt of it. An excuse to get in, nonetheless," Pauline said.

"What's your favorite color?" The question became abrupt and pointed, but Monica put her hand on her head and waited for an answer.

"Blood red, I guess," she said, looking down at the pool of red liquid and dipping the last of the cake into it.

"We're going to get along. I want to find out more about you, find out more about our girls…We really must temper the girls, especially when they bicker."

"Oh, let them bicker. They're better for it. It won't ruin my vacation," Pauline said.

They both laughed.

"Who was your favorite significant other?" Pauline asked, trying to ask just as daring of a question.

"I guess my last. I had a guy I dated briefly. Sometimes I have an itch I need to satisfy, you know?"

"I do; I do." But Pauline didn't quite act in those moments of indecision. She had become more and more repulsed by men coming on to her since she turned sixty. She remembered the birthday so well. A man. A cheap suit. His arm outstretched above her shoulder asking her if she liked opera. He knew nothing about opera.

"He was so soft. I could boss him around. You know. It was glorious. Make the bed. Bring me coffee. Do this in bed…" Monica's had trailed off, and she limply flitted her hand in the air. She paused and looked straight at Pauline. "Oh well, I eventually got bored."

"Is there anything you want to do on vacation?" Monica asked.

"Well," she said. She took a sip of water and looked in the other direction. "I guess I don't want to hike in the woods. So, there's that. But I'll like the wineries and the long drives around the lakes. I'll like the ambiance and the company for sure." She grabbed Monica's hand. "Don't stress. This will be fun…or else." She made a loose fist and shook it to show she was serious.

"I love you already." Monica winked.

"What are your hopes and dreams, Monica?"

"Well, I'm a People Magazine and meatloaf girl. A big night out includes going for ice cream or taking a walk around the block. I guess I'm like you, single and ready to mingle," Monica said. "My ex-husband is a wanted man, an evil man. He abused dogs for Christ's sake. Not worth anyone's time. I'm so glad I kicked him to the curb. It took a lot to go to the domestic shelter and meet with a social worker. I started over. Life took a course, and nobody liked it. It was a long time ago when Casey could barely tie her shoes."

"Oh, Monica. I'm so sorry. It didn't occur to me." Pauline thought back about her own life and trials and tribulations, which couldn't even compare.

"He lifted a hard hand, and I complied for a long time. He tunneled me in. No one had a place for me to go, but I got out and I'm alive. Oh baby, I am alive and ready for a new man."

"I'm so happy for you. That you turned your life around and things are stable."

"Kick them to the curb if they are one of those wicked men."

"That's the only way to do it," Pauline said, joining in her celebration of life after the breakup.

In an instant, a broad smile came across Monica's face. "I'm ready for an adventure. I've always wanted to go on a cruise. I'd be all in…" Monica inhaled. "We might take off to see the world next." Monica cocked her head, and Pauline knew she had posed a question.

"Oh Monica," Pauline said. "I will show you things and places."

"Oh, please do, Pauline. I'm ready for anything. Bring it on." She extended her arm and pulled a fisted hand back at her chest, almost uncharacteristically.

Pauline thought the motion was daring and savory. Monica was ready for anything and that was exactly what Pauline needed, someone craving adventure at the same rate as her.

"Monica, you are so very…absolutely…the best. We will find fun."

The absence of a check made them stay a little longer than they would have. They had no clue about leaving. They linked elbows and made their way to the door. "All in suitable time," Pauline thought, "I will corrupt her." Pauline laughed a bit maniacally to herself and straightened her blouse.

Before they parted, they hugged outside the door. They had rushed out, passing the maître de, as the restaurant pulled the curtains to mark its opening. This venture was in its second week. Pauline knew people. Monica gathered that much. They promised each other they would behave as Pauline took Monica's biceps strongly in her hands. They would become the best of friends, in fact, was what Monica responded. They would keep those girls in line, and have them do what they wanted to do, be vocal about their interests. They would not let the girls take too much control.

"Just don't tell the girls. They don't need to be told about our date. How else were we supposed to know if the trip would work?" Pauline asked.

Monica gave a smile and said, "Hmph."

Pauline knew she was right.

When Pauline gave Monica a kiss on the cheek before turning swiftly in the other direction, it caught Monica off-guard. She twisted her head and moved in another direction. Pauline was simply fancy. That was all she meant. Perhaps it overwhelmed Monica. She caught herself breathing more rapidly, possibly out of embarrassment, before she also turned and walked away, wondering about Monica and the party she would be at tonight. Whether there would be the same cake, or at least something at the end of the night with a cherry glaze.

Monica moseyed over to her car, and Pauline watched, almost like a mother, to make sure it started, and she got off okay. She watched Monica put on her seat belt, fix her hair, and smack her lips. She started up the car and made her way down the street, only noticing Pauline was still watching when she passed right next to the entrance of the restaurant.

Pauline looked back through the window to see Robert picking up the remnants of what they had left. Only a few crumbs remained on the plate. He stacked the dishes, doing the dirty work of a busser on behalf of his good friends. He had no shame.

CHAPTER 2

Tera kicked up her stride forcefully. The activity relieved stress. She hadn't run in quite a while, but she signed up for a race and had to beat the times she had made a few years ago. She would never say that stress tortured her, but it did. A run gave her focus. When she woke up, she was sometimes angry first thing as she thought about the day to come, and at so many points throughout the day she had this unbridled energy; she couldn't stand still. If she was tired, though, things were manageable. So, this was how she managed her stress. Get out into the world and exercise all the guidance said. So she did. She did it to relieve stress and the sickly-sweet sweat. She took breaks and went for walks at work. She did all the things she needed to do to have better mental health and to take care of herself.

Abruptly, a loud clap issued from a house on Tera's right side. It sounded like a gunshot, and she paused when she probably should've moved to a full sprint. Her arms hung limp from exertion, and she heaved. Running fatigue and the loud noise had scared her to a stop. A garage door had fallen. A man appeared and muddled about scratching his head as if wondering what the next step was. He had no one to ask.

She leaped into a sprint to the finish. She pushed harder as sweat began pouring from her forehead. The wetness stuck her shirt to her chest. This was exhilaration. This amounted to fun. "Hardly," she thought. But the stiff direction, the call to action, pushed her toward the finish.

She slowed for a moment before snapping back to her goal. Again, she sprinted, checking her watch, and panting through the elongated five minutes before she relaxed to a canter to recover. These intervals, meant to increase her stamina, killed her spirit. Again.

When she passed a man with a dog mulling about, she felt

a glob of snot brewing in her sniffling nose. She hocked the mucus into her mouth and spit. The man responded in kind, spitting next to his dog relieving himself on a tree in the sidewalk. No offense taken.

These were the days before the trial by fire, the test of wills. She and her mom and her girlfriend and her girlfriend's mom were going on vacation. This was why she began running. Running away from the entire event. It caused Tera so much heartburn. Her face twisted in disgust when Casey brought it up. And yet, they were going. The journey would happen. In more than a few ways, it would be a test of fate. And Tera never, ever left anything up to fate. That's why she considered it particularly agitating.

Casey and Tera were having issues. It became the second heartburn, heartache. As much as she wanted it to work, things took time. They tussled with words more than twice a week: after a nice dinner, before a movie date, on the phone, or at a friend's house.

Tera didn't want to be alone. She would've broken it off and ended the whole thing, the whole affair. She cherished her alone time when she needed a break from Casey, a recharge. That much became true. But every day in and out she knew led to basic restlessness, loneliness, lying in bed until 1:00 p.m. on a Saturday afternoon. She couldn't handle that. She was sure.

Yet, this date with the moms, a full week's vacation no less, was a step toward commitment. Marriage, no less, was looming, and it was nerve-wracking. They weren't ready. They hadn't prepared adequately. Their relationship needed more solidity. "What if their moms didn't like each other? What if they fought in front of their moms? What if someone got too drunk and told stories?"

Tera had stories. She stopped running and put her hands on her knees, heaved in and out and tried to find normalcy in her breath. She could not think, and as the memories came leaping back out, she breathed heavier. Her actions wouldn't allow her to gain composure.

She remembered Mark, merely a local guy. They got into trouble almost every day. Not quite a boyfriend, not quite a someone she didn't make out with. His hair protruded stiff but greasy. It stuck in one direction and not necessarily ever the same direction again. His nose, awkwardly broken and reset twice, resulted from fights with the kids at school.

He got into fights. Some considered him a bruiser, and she liked it…for a bit. Her mom did not. Tera hid everything. She couldn't bring him home. That proved true. When they went off gallivanting, they got into trouble.

Only now did Tera consider herself a terrible daughter. She had done what she did and now she tried to give it all some justice through a half-cocked plan to make up for incidents about ten years ago. She reformed herself without reform school. Her best manners faced forward, despite never having gone to finishing school. She apologized with actions for past events. She only hoped it worked. Her mom who whined, "I was such a negligent mother," three times a week. Tera would make things right. Fix everything that happened because of her unruly behavior.

With a happy clip in her step, she started into the driveway. She had done the loop she set out to do. She had plotted the course for Sundays, and the day came round. Her mind pulsed, intending to do it, and she did intervals even. All to prep for an upcoming race. This test of endurance and willpower became her last step in getting away from the demons of her teenage years. She had come full circle and now coasted into a better place. She counted it as true.

She grabbed a towel at the door to the house and wiped beading sweat from her forehead, her chest, under her arms. The smell wafted from her pits. She needed a shower, but Casey lay awake and excited to see her. This was a rare-bird morning where she had gone for a run. Usually, she saved them for the afternoon or evening. Casey finally woke up somewhat early and Tera, fatigued, fought off tiredness. The crankiness would come.

She must take a shower right away. That's what she did.

The steam came in, and she adjusted her spine. For so many years, she hated gym class. She wouldn't touch sports. Here she was a model of herself and what she might be. She was a woman with a stable, decent job, what she thought was a proud parent. And a girlfriend with a hot body. Nothing better. She couldn't find a reason to look any further. If she could simply coast out the rest of her life like this, she would find satiation. She would have achieved an unnamed goal, become the antithesis of who she became ten years ago, a nemesis version of herself.

The suds coated her body. Sometimes in the steam she forgot up and down, where she placed feet on the ground, and what treatment she needed to apply: shampoo, conditioner, or soap. She would shampoo twice or forget to rinse her hair. The steam capsized her. Into a flashback or a dream-like state she would go, remembering, imagining. The warmth, the clean sweat, intoxicated and triggered all at the same time. She became who she had never been and loose in all things she now kept tightly organized, planned, and calculated.

The steam beaded new cold sweat on her forehead. It cooled her forehead as the hot water poured in. The fog of steam got dense as she realized she hadn't put on the fan. She tightened her fists at her overlooked action. Soon, in came memories of things that pestered, persisted.

In the shower, in a vision of the past, she saw herself with the boy over the dead body. They looked down at the shell of a man too young to be called as much. Mark kicked at the dirt, but Tera thought he nailed the body. She pushed him back, and he slammed into the ground. They fought with words. He yelled from his seated position up at Tera, who knew she was right. Better, would turn it in. Mark's voice boomed. Won. Its deepness rounded whole smothering Tera's body. Winning. They would never find this place again out in the woods where they had made trouble.

She saw these figures: Mark, a body, and someone like her. It wasn't her, though. She held her breath. She watched herself reenact the events. The leaves on the ground flitted around lightly in the air. They circled into a tornado and the body wrenched in, removed from the ground, twisted up into the air until it escaped in the clouds.

In the instant, Tera fell flat back to the ground, and Mark rose. He looked down at her body and mouthed the words, "I loved you." Tera crossed her arms across her chest, as if in a coffin ready for burial. She tried as she might, and they wouldn't move.

Tera slammed the shower handle down as she imploded in the vision. She jammed the door open to get a towel. She had too much.

Tera wiped her eyes deep with the towel. She had remembered this several times before, but this was the first time it had overtaken her, so she had to stop it. The steam and the heat fostered her illusion until it dissipated. She rubbed her feet on the wet bathmat.

CHAPTER 3

"Cup of coffee?" Casey asked. "I popped down the road to get cream this morning. You absolutely need it." Her smile gleamed in the bright light of the morning.

Anyone could see their radiant love if they were only there at that moment. But it was only the two of them, and Tera didn't see the lust from the love, from the friendship they had for so long. The smile curled under. The sunlight obscured the face. She couldn't see the love in the air, the impending vacation.

Casey returned to the room with a mug. Tera had given the heart mug to her for valentine's day one year. She got it cheap but filled it with a gift card to one of Tera's favorite bookstores. The mug, a corny tribute of a gift, often sat a centerpiece on the kitchen table, unused. But Tera loved romance novels, so be it. Casey sat down and pushed it toward her. Tera didn't take it at first, but then stole sips from the delicate edge, positioning her lips ninety degrees past a chip that surfaced some several months ago.

"Is this your bra?" Casey held up her hand and let it drop almost in an instant. She took another drag off the mug.

Casey and Tera approached their mid-twenties, but they had moved in together a few weeks ago. Their relationship, stitched together lightly, didn't verge on marriage, but they had taken a leap. They could always find another place, and they would work out the lease. A replacement apartment was easy enough to get. Despite all this, they rented a huge, assuming townhouse in a crisp, clean spectacle of a neighborhood.

Tera adjusted the waist of her jeans. "They're our bras." Tera slid a snide smile across her face. They both agreed. Casey borrowed them often. Oh, hers lingered in the wash. Oh, hers must be behind the dresser. That this would lead to their demise was a conjecture, but in the same respect, partially true.

"Casey. I'll buy you some, tell me which ones." She picked at her nails as she often did. Her structured amber bob ran an inch past her chin, and she often curled the ends up around her ears. Then, when they hung loose, the curl would stick with a rounded character, giving her hair depth.

"You know what it is," Casey said.

"Do I? I don't think we've hashed this out before." Tera's anger rose and subsided with Casey's calmness, her nonchalance.

"We have separate rooms now."

Tera needed space. She needed to rest her back and flail freely in the rising morning light. Moreover, Casey tossed and turned fiercely as soon as the sun peaked out from the trees and often could not get back to sleep and could not get up. She said she feared the cold, empty room in the morning.

"It's so childish. It's not haunted," Tera had said.

"I want to be close to you, that's all." She took a sweeping gulp and drank the coffee in a desperate chug. It fell at her side, and she balanced the handle between her fingers loosely, jerking every so often to make sure it was still there.

Tera let out a deep sigh. They were getting too close. The lesbian tendency to merge had taken over two years ago right away when they met, and now they were distancing. They had gone too far. They had fallen in love, and the emotions rambled. Tera had put her coat around Casey for the first time two weeks in. Her hair got shorter, much like Tera's two weeks later. They had moved in together much too soon. They spent all their time together. Were they now uncoupling in small steps, small words that drove a stake in deeper? Tera, most definitively, wiggled it around, pulled on the wedge, creating a larger gap.

Casey shoved it in her suitcase, glancing back at Tera.

Tera saw her disappointment, her frustration.

The women continued to pack. The moms would be ready tomorrow. They had packed a week ago. They likely anticipated the trip much more than "the girls." Perhaps their conception was more of excitement; Tera elicited more or less trepidation.

"What are you most nervous about?" Casey asked. Her smile grew broad.

"I guess I want everyone to enjoy themselves. Our moms will not fight how we might fight. I'm sure they'll get along. My mom is so nice, and your mom is so appropriate. But if we fight, the moms might not have a good time. It might all be a bad idea. We won't know until the end, until it's over," Tera said.

Tera always had a little apprehension about being in her mom's presence for more than a few hours. Even when the family, full of energy, gathered up steam, packed up everything in sight, and started up the car ready for vacations, she receded to her cozy room. She would opt out of family events. That might've been, Tera thought sometimes, how it all started. She had grown up that way and here she was decades later, still uneasy about spending a long week with her mom and, to top it off, her girlfriend's mom. She needed to impress, and she wasn't sure if she could, given that she and her mom had a very frank relationship.

"I'm scared my mom will be the only one who talks. You know how she had kooky conversations, asks things like, 'what's your favorite animal?' and 'what are you most nervous about?' She really tries to keep people talking but sometimes goes too far. So, that's it for me. I worry Monica, who I will never call Monica to her face, will be overzealous about politics or anything really and extra gabby," Casey said.

"Oh, she won't. My mom will love it. She will engage and chat. She'll keep them both under control," Tera said.

"My mom gets so excited and talks so much. But your mom intimidates her. Her money does. So, she might be apprehensive. I simply hope—"

"Don't belabor it, Casey. It'll be fine. You're obsessing."

They planned the trip in February, and tomorrow they would leave on a cool June day, planned with Pauline's hot flashes in mind. It would be mild in the Finger Lakes in June. They hadn't made it a July vacation or gone south because Pauline would glaze over in wetness on an even, warm spring day. She sweated when they were hiking and when they relaxed on a patio eating dinner in the summer sun. It was only that's the way it was. She needed to keep hydrated.

Tera and Casey gathered things out of the drawer, quietly, loosely folding them. Nothing really needed to be ironed or wrinkle free. They would not go to a wedding or event, but they might go eat at a restaurant a few times to let the moms act like proper adults. Moms always liked to have their silverware arranged correctly.

"I'm going to go get the last load of laundry," Casey said. "The basement beckons. I'll get the extra coffee and water from the stock shelves, too. Do you need anything?"

"No. I'm fine." She kept her answer brief and followed it as a quick air-kiss, even though the tinge of Tera's anger pushed through. This vacation would be a test. It was a be-all-end-all, their bonding. With their mothers in tow, they would find out what it meant to be together as a family. Their parents' traits would eventually be their own. "Would they like each other in twenty years, at middle age, at the end of life?" These glimpses would let them confront the inevitable and who they each really were. If they didn't get through this. The uncoupling would begin.

Tera continued to pack while Casey was in the basement and the kitchen, gathering things together. Twice as much coffee as usual. Two times the mac and cheese. The extra-large soup pot. Two instead of one bag of chips.

Tera folded and finished and worked on Casey's bag. She'd repack it for sure. But it was the only way Tera could thank Casey at this moment in time. Casey might repack it. Pull everything out, question what Tera had done, and throw things back in unfolded. Tera picked out the clothes anyway and zipped up the bag. She put it by the door but didn't bring it down to the kitchen to load it just yet.

On the edge of the bed, Tera looked into the mostly

empty coffee cup and swirled a last bit of the dregs, casting it aside on the bed after a last swig. She leaned back on stiff arms, bumping her chest out, wishing Casey were there. Wishing she was pushing herself into her. Making up, melting anger to passion, forgetting the years and also remembering them.

When Casey returned, she expressed similar sentiments. She entered the room, stopped, and stared. In a low, quiet tone, she introduced her side. "This is really it. This is our last shot. I'm sorry it must be with our mom's, but we will find a way out of it all. It's going to be difficult because the qualities I have that annoy you are also my mom's and vice versa. Let's try to be our best for our moms. When we get back, we can complain about it all and 'uncouple' as you say if we need to. Let's act appropriate, smile all the time, and ask them questions. Listen. Just give me that." Her smile poked loosely out of the corner of her mouth, almost forced there. It quivered as she held it.

They'd been fighting recently. She counted the knock-down, drag-out fights. No one would deny that they fought like banshees and had sex like sirens. The lumps of laundry lying around the house, in the hall, the bedroom, the office created a fire in Tera's eyes. Casey had stopped caring months ago. This one last barrier broke Tera's sound mind. Meanwhile, Tera had become raucous watching sports all day. She had a new sport every week. This week she started pickup games at a local court, knee deep in pickle ball. The week before, she hung out on the couch watching soccer for research on her client at work. Sounded more like research for herself than her client. That's what Casey said, anyway. What she thought was likely much, much worse. It would sway their relationship in not so many words.

The staples, football, baseball, golf, and hockey ran on replay throughout the day. Those regular showings morphed Tera into a separate being. There'd be hollering and laughs. Even in solitude, she relished the sweet sweat of others. Somehow keeping herself amused. Visibly keeping herself amused.

Tera called Casey lazy a week ago. Tera sprawled on the couch, chips between her legs, told her how she saw it. She said it off-hand and softly, mumbling as she had been to herself for weeks. It seemed like that was the first stage of failure. What she held inside was coming out. The words would become more lucid, more real. As she slowly voiced them, she would tap into more hidden sensations, thoughts, and anger. Their attitudes and behaviors made them both sick at times, but they both thought it would get better. They'd get past the worst of it.

Not today, Tera repeated to herself. Not this week. Too much could go wrong. She wouldn't miss this chance, or the relationship would go south. The mom wouldn't like her, and it was over. She would keep her daughter from her and all that they had invested. The moms had paid a portion as well. They couldn't get a refund at this point. It would be an ordeal if they had to cancel. They were going…tally ho. She wouldn't ruin this relationship by running or finking out, giving up the second things got a little hot.

CHAPTER 4

Pauline fiddled with the buttons on Tera's jacket. She dipped her hand into a bag of buttons to find a replica. After several tries, she found one that more or less matched, somehow. Serendipity. She promised to have it done for Tera by the time of the trip. Even though it was just about summer. Even though she wouldn't need the jacket until the fall at the earliest. She promised. She would deliver. Pauline was talented with so many things. Despite that, she had always wanted to be as good as her mother at sewing. She would sew her own clothes. Sew Pauline's. She cooked up rare delicacies with flair and wonder in the kitchen. She was the stay-at-home parent of the century. Pauline still had her mother's apron cast across a hook in her kitchen. She could never bring herself to use it.

Maybe Pauline wished she was like her mother and never could be. Pauline tried to be the stay-at-home parent of the century. The mother of the century. Still, her husband dumped her. Her daughter dumped her. Here she was though, her daughter was taking her on a trip, making up for lost time, apologizing in a way, potentially. And she had a brand-new convertible.

From the bag of buttons, Pauline picked out a gold button with an anchor on it. She rubbed her hands over it as if it were a smooth beach pebble. She would take it with her in her pocket and rub it every time she had a worry or some anxiety about her daughter. She was acting as an exemplary mother should, sewing for her daughter. Actions sometimes meant more than words.

A devilish thought crossed her mind. Her alter ego, her evil self, plotted to rip all the buttons off the coat and sew on odd and unique buttons, a purple marble, a brass military button, or a red clown nose button in the center. Oh, how

Tera would freak. She laughed to herself, giggling mischievously. Tera would go berserk. Trivial things kept Pauline amused. She was a terrible mother.

Pauline pricked her finger and struggled with a thimble to resolve the problem. Her own mother had taught her how to sew. Despite being a little prim and proper, she did domestic things. Although she was more than capable of going down to the dry cleaners and paying for it to be professionally done, she took on the task herself. I will never do it quite as well as my mother. She pulled the thread through loosely, almost purposefully, not tightening it the whole way. She too needed to understand being needed. If Tera complained, she'd do it again. She had so much time before fall.

"Tera was such a moody daughter," Pauline thought. Still to this day, she answered the phone, almost growling, "What?" Daughters could be moody when they entered their teenage years. And Tera came out in full bloom, rattling everyone with mere words. But Pauline still counted her as family, always would. After all these years, Tera pined for a vacation. Imagine that. She could apologize with a trip and be nice and cordial, but the moodiness shined through: the passive aggressiveness and the snide comments. Actions didn't amount to more than words.

But Pauline considered herself a horrible parent. That's what she always told herself. Absent and ruthless, she stalked the halls, waiting to deal discipline she never dealt. She never let Tera have any freedom. That's why she was so rebellious as a teenager. She told herself this repeatedly, flogging herself with a cat of nine tails over and over. She took responsibility for her daughter's behavior, Tera's rebellion, that Tera smoked and hung out late at night with boys. Her grades dropped, and her father left them. Both things she tied together as her fault. If she didn't have dinner at the table, even if she wasn't sure if Tera would come home at night or not, it would have been different. Passive aggressiveness. An adult acting out. The blame rested with her.

Still, Pauline admitted that somehow, after years of being

absent from her mom, Tera had turned out all right. Organized and forthright, and she planned for things with a meticulous nature and, thankfully, considered others. She had done a complete one-eighty. Or, she had simply just grown up. At face value, she was an upstanding citizen. Unfortunately, if you spent more than a half hour with her, her genuine attitude came out, and she could get nasty.

Pauline always thought about Tera and Mark. She thought those two would go to hell together. They were inseparable. Mark always had a smile for Pauline when she saw him, but she knew the devious intentions that lurked behind that smile. She knew his true self. She knew Robert anyway, and they were spitting images. Smiles and fanfare, but behind closed doors, all bets were off.

Mark was Robert's and Samantha's child. That boy got into trouble as soon as someone put their eyes on him. Pauline had known it from the beginning. Still, she let her daughter get close to him and then pushed them together when Tera started to withdraw and became depressed. She saw how happy they were together and thought that was the only way to make things better.

Of course, Tera was gay.

Of course, Pauline loved Robert and Samantha. Through the thick and thin of it, she cherished them as her best friends. Nothing could tear all three of them apart. Pauline became the third wheel after her husband left, but the couple always made her warm with welcome, as if they had all three always been together. She was so grateful for those years, Tera's teenage years and Pauline's mid-life. It filled them with emotion, abandonment, and tears, but also the best of friends. Pauline and Tera both were friends formed in turmoil.

At one point, Robert, Samantha, and Mark left for a vacation. They made off for the Berkshires in eighty-dollar polos and linen slacks. Yoga, hiking, all that earthy stuff. Robert still worked his corporate job as a lawyer at that point.

The three vacationers had two open bedrooms in the

house and invited Pauline and her daughter to join them. Of course, Pauline understood she would only spend time together in the house. Her aversion to hiking was clear. She didn't even like yoga. "She'd try it," she thought to herself. But she forgot a mat. Uncanny.

The vacation didn't flop. Everyone had a raucous time. Robert and Samantha took time during the day to bond. Pauline did some luxurious hot tubbing on someone else's bill. To be fair, she bought all the groceries and paid for gas. The superstar couple footed the bill for the place.

When they returned, drinks and card games covered the tables. They had steaks on the grill, or Robert would whip something up. He would spend all day on a large piece of pork. The steam would rise. Clouds of smoke poured through the house. Robert disengaged the smoke alarm and pulled out the battery. His work, true calling, made itself heard. The next summer, he quit his job. This was his mid-life crisis, or a second look at what his life had become. The first being when he quit Samantha unexpectedly. He came back four weeks later to a devastated house. He quit and started culinary school, traveled to Italy. Spent the summer in Italy without Samantha.

All the while, unbeknownst to the rest of the group, the kids took the car. No one understood where they hid or what they did to occupy themselves. Considered good kids at fifteen and sixteen, Tera and Mark took advantage of a long leash. That first summer, Mark turned sixteen and Tera couldn't catch up, still fifteen. They didn't get into trouble at first. It all started off so well, so doomed for success for all five of them.

She wrapped up the sewing kit and tied a ribbon around it. Her mom tied knotted ribbons in her hair, age eight, and tears dripped bloody murder. Every day, her mom would dress up her hair in this one ribbon. Here it was after so long, holding together an old and used sewing kit. Pauline slipped the sewing kit in her cedar dresser drawer. Her mom wouldn't be so proud, she thought. There were imperfections in her, and Tera's lives, their history. Yet still she would smile that Pauline, after all these years, while having so much money, continued to sew with her mother's sewing kit.

CHAPTER 5

Pauline put on her best slacks and blouse. She chose a belt not quite the same camel color as her wide-leg trousers, and a silver necklace to complement her blue Ralph Lauren top. Looking at herself in the mirror, she fluffed the pieces, which were not as expensive as she would've liked. She wished she were a little more to-do, wealthier, but since she and Arnold officially split, she didn't quite have as much money. She hoped for a Hermes bag for a long time. Arnold might've bought it for her—to control her. He would've demanded sex for weeks. She only had the beat-up Kate Spade. She got it at an outlet, no less. They split the retirement in half. They both downsized on a house. The Kate Spade was enough.

Anthony, a chef of some regard, had invited Pauline to his party as a nice courtesy. Both she and Anthony understood this. Pauline would probably say the wrong thing. Pauline would be quiet. Of course, Robert would enter through a cold door alone, but so would Samantha, his ex. She knew this. She and Robert wouldn't go together. It couldn't happen. She plunged the knife into their friendship the moment Samantha left. Moments and weeks before, Robert must've known they would sever.

Pauline hated that she couldn't tell Anthony that she couldn't relay the news sooner. Samantha fell swiftly out of a stable relationship and drowned in a lustful partnership. With a woman. He wouldn't likely recover for some time.

Samantha, a food and wine writer of much acclaim, would survive this break-up and likely the one she was having currently with her girlfriend. Pauline teetered, unsure if this new relationship would last, but she was sure Samantha wouldn't go back to Robert. She couldn't. She had done too much damage, and she knew it.

Pauline, Robert, and Samantha came together once as

friends. They were all going separately now to have a delight-ful time. The host agreed to have Pauline there as well, even though limited seating prevented more guests, because he wanted a fresh palate, one unaffected with the drama and gossip of the food world in their little city. Pauline thought it was simply to have someone speak well of it all because that's exactly what she would do from inexperience. Having an immature pallet could be a good thing. It could also backfire. Pauline expected only the best but didn't dare guess what she'd do if she didn't like something.

Pauline had sashayed into Robert's restaurant because of what she had to tell him. That Samantha wouldn't come back, ever. She said it with her eyes, even if her words were less harsh. They would go their way and, after this first dinner event apart, probably never speak again. They would run into each other at events, just words would not issue, elbows would not rub. From each other, to each other, at least. Other people, influencers, would surely talk.

Pauline was going to Anthony's party stag. Keep the look subdued. She didn't care. Robert and his ex were also solo, Samantha. Samantha left Robert in a whirlwind. She met the love of her life and carried it on for about three to four weeks; she was working late at the office, a trite excuse that a man would use when he was out all night with his secretary. On the weekend, she worked out at the gym more than usu-al—to get herself in shape for her husband.

All the while, she dated Sal, a butch lesbian who came right out of a time when being gay was so dangerous. Her hair and demeanor were some thirty years dated. Pauline was sure Samantha liked the edge. She must've liked the danger and evasion of her husband. Pauline, she laughed inwardly, thought she might scream out during an orgasm in the gen-eral direction of her home, where Robert was, to spite him, to have an explosive orgasm.

When she entered the room to the party of about twenty, she checked the watch and then the clock on the wall. She sucked her lips into her teeth. She left her bag and light coat in the first-floor bedroom, where the door cracked open. A pile of coats stood ready to topple. Pauline put hers on the side and said a quick prayer that she wouldn't make a scene.

An accessible house provided so much security for the future. To be older and stuck in something that didn't work would cause so much effort to rectify. Without Arnold, she wouldn't have been able to get that beautiful one floor rancher they had decided on getting when they were together. She would have enough for a clunky 1950s place that needed a lot of upkeep, painting, and power washing, weeding and driveway repaving. She would never get to that place now.

The dining room had one or two open seats, and she confirmed her seat through a place card. Robert sat opposite Samantha. Someone probably switched their place cards when one of them arrived without the other. The single presence was likely explained in quiet breaths. Anthony's spouse, Ryan, a young sprig of a thing, probably switched the cards. His eye for detail was impeccable. Pauline hoped Samantha was the one to bring it up with Anthony that she had gone out and got another lover. Careened over the internet looking for a spouse. Googled dictionaries of terms so she wouldn't look dumb or uninformed. She took Pauline to get a vibrator at the sex shop. They parked out back with the rest of the cars and entered the windowless building together, hoping to avoid the truckers. They marketed the stop toward other seedy folks.

The gay bars used to not have windows. Pauline noticed that many years ago when she puttered around about not ready wander in. Now, when the bars were in new buildings, which they sometimes were, the windows were less shaded, or open. It was easier to see into them. The gay coffee shops and bookstores didn't have that same shutdown aura, one that made you question if they were ever open.

They left the heads of the table empty. Each place is a lucky spot in the minds of anyone outside the room but in the world of food. A place card identified who should be at which seat. This simply prevented intruders from joining the party. It did, in fact, not and several people had lined up out-side to get into the party.

Robert, midway down the table, two seats away from Samantha's spot on the opposite side, sat as a heavy mass. He grabbed at the edge of the table to steady himself, glancing at Pauline, in her direction. Samantha showed up sometime later, Sans new partner, girlfriend, or triste. But the guests issued words. People asked about her, the woman. Pauline could hardly imagine what ran through Robert's head, but the word partner probably floated around in there. Robert stead-ied himself because he could all but cry out to Pauline for help.

They ran through the courses at a gallop. The first taste, a fig amuse-bouche, soaked in a rhubarb jam, wet pallets. Applause ensued after the first bite. An unanticipated encore followed. Pauline couldn't figure what the next one was, a gel-like liquid with a round berry on top, clear, greenish. This second bite, entirely unlike the other, unrecognizable, left the crowd with jaws dropped muttering. The sweet crisp flavor reminded Pauline instantly of the blood red pool in the dessert she had at lunch. They served ceviche and Broccoli Raab separately. An oddly paired meatloaf followed. Pauline knew that much that it was much too heavy to follow broc-coli. A tiny steak with glaze and mushrooms followed the supposed main course. She ate the steak more willingly and thought nothing of the cut, though hers might've been the best. The cake served at the end mimicked the one she ate with Monica. She absolutely could not eat it, with her full belly bellowing to relax.

Monica dressed in plain pleasant fashion and her attitude matched to the same beat. She came from a clan of clean and hardworking people and lived in a rural area but commuted to the city center for her job at the bank. A finance expert, she worked with numbers and statistics, never as a teller. The local bank didn't pay what other financial offices paid, but she said she considered herself happy to not be in the rat race. Said she liked it. It could've all been for appearances.

Monica was an amiable woman so far. She hadn't revealed too much. Still, she initiated every conversation with a bit of elusiveness, a bit of reserve, and leering eyes. She ended most sentences with an actual hiss, trailing her s's and leering as if she didn't believe it was all true. She recanted her skepticism about her gay daughter and being friends with her daughter's girlfriend's single mom. To Pauline, uniqueness should be celebrated. She cherished it. The absurdity of it all, the hilarity.

Pauline would crack her shell for sure. It would be a challenge, but she was confident she could do it. She would find out who this Monica might be, how her daughter and she interacted and affected each other. What made each react? How proud was she?

She sat alone, solo, trying to concentrate on taking another bite, one she would never take.

"Oh, you look lonely," one guest said.

She had a polka dotted pashmina thrown over her neck. The fringes sat in front of her, just waiting to be dipped in soup. A long flowing skirt saw she matched the occasion. Perhaps more so than Pauline did. She didn't dress for the food writing community. Instead, she might make for an office party or even a low-key meeting.

"Oh, not really so lonely, just low," Pauline said.

Losing friendship with Samantha and Robert devastated Pauline. In fact, she had lost them both when they lost each other. Samantha barely ever called. Robert only had one goal and Pauline was the conduit, which made Samantha distance herself more from Robert. Stuck, she resigned herself to that point. By this moment, she might declare she needed new friends.

"Hi. Let me start over. I'm Pauline," she said.

"Nice to meet you Pauline, I'm Kay," she said. "I saw you sitting over here so glum. I'm afraid you need a friend." She settled into the seat they erroneously assigned her beside Pauline now that eaters had dispersed, got up to talk and digest. She leaned into Pauline. "I'm friends with Samantha. You are as well?"

"Yes. Yes. I am friends with Samantha and—" She didn't

need another link to something she meant to create distance from.

"What's up with her and Robert?" Kay followed. "There is so much tension here tonight."

"Tell me about it," Pauline said.

Pauline scrambled for words. She didn't want to get into this at this party. Relaxing her arm on the chair, she pulled her other forearm across her stomach. She was ready to leave and turned to apologize. Her stomach had turned, and her purpose didn't include upsetting the host, but she had to leave.

When Pauline got up to leave, she dusted some crumbs off her lap. Robert and Samantha had still not spoken. She sat in silence, still picking at crumbs, trying to look occupied while others spoke about food and eating around her. A few minutes too early to leave, she roamed about, glancing up and smiling, all with an angered stomach.

She thought back to her date with Monica. The dear woman pulled through the room with grace, head held high. Monica inherently couldn't be as worldly as Pauline herself. She had a few silver-capped teeth, and her clothes were unimpressive. . She was tidy and neat. The good qualities stood out to Pauline. She was chatty, but nice. Sweet Monica started conversations quickly and rarely ended a topic, always adding trailing thoughts. Strikingly, in that small town, their circles had never crossed. None of their friends mingled with each other. Pauline was happy to, though, have met Monica and call her a friend.

Pauline wondered what Monica would do in a situation like this. And as she thought it, alone, the only person still sitting picking at food, so wished she were here with her. She wished they could continue their casual conversation and warm up to each other. She longed for a good friend, and potentially that's what Monica could be. Pauline wished she had a best friend. She had to side with Robert, the original friend. Samantha was out of the picture. Caught in the middle, she was without a devoted friend altogether.

Against her better judgment, Pauline would go home and

go to sleep. She wouldn't call Monica to fill her in, even though she really wanted to talk about how she couldn't have even one more bite of cake.

She rose, a shadow, and made her way to the first-floor bedroom. A spiral staircase led to a lower level. As she peered down, she could see sculptures and paintings. Pauline wondered and hoped that the room wouldn't flood. They surely would heed the warnings of a hurricane if it came up the east coast. Losing the artwork would be major.

She gathered her coat from the pile, thanked the hosts, and complimented the meal. She promised to compose her thoughts and email with reviews on each dish. Of course, he wouldn't post them anywhere. Pauline didn't write, but the gracious gesture flattered her. Other critics in the room spoke freely and continued to chat about what they liked best, what was a little uninspired, and how they would change things. Robert and Samantha did so as well, just in opposite corners of the room.

Pauline pulled the top down on her convertible before she pulled out of the well-lit neighborhood. The warm days came in growing spring day by spring day, but the evenings were consistently cool. The May showers kept the temperature of the soil down. She wanted to readdress her suitcase, what she packed.

This truly would be the trip of all trips. The couple fought profusely when Tera was in her teens, but it all worked out after Tera came out to her and her friends. Tera didn't want any temper tantrums. She wanted all the information, all the time, when she wanted it. Pauline walked on glass to not upset her. She just hoped with Casey she had tamed her emotions a bit more. It surely would've been a feat years ago, but Tera hardly spent time with Casey, real bonding time. This was truly a chance, and Tera had jumped at it, other mother-in-law in tow or not.

CHAPTER 6

The grocery store held ten lost souls on a Thursday at 7:00 p.m. Pauline thought people would've been bustling about getting ready for cookouts and buying food for weekend parties. Instead, it was inanely quiet. No one seemed to make a fuss at the register. No one tried to pull a box out of the bottom of a display, and an ample number of stockers were moving about. She stopped someone to inquire about where she could find Mexican food. Inevitably, she would go to the wrong aisle.

Designers set most grocery stores up the same. They included a produce section as you entered. Pauline thought cheerfully that encouraging veggies in your diet takes all precedence, but it also must've been the greens and freshness that drew people in, reminded them that junk food was not the be all end all. The fresh food would also go bad quicker, so why shouldn't the store make a first push to sell that food? The bread and milk were always together. Staples for convenience, sometimes near a bakery. The meat lined the back of the store in freezer cases. Snacks were usually in the second to last aisle. That's how architects set most stores up. That's what Pauline had always understood about grocery stores, except for a few specialty stores or the big wholesaler store she'd been in once.

Tera surfaced somewhere around the bananas after parking the car.

"There's got to be a way to refill those tiny ketchup bottles. Isn't there, really? I mean, if I get this large ketchup bottle, I could squirt it into the small one, right?" Pauline said.

"Mom, just bring the large ketchup bottle. There's four of us," Tera said.

"Sure. But it's waste not want not; you see?" She stared

hard into Tera's eyes and almost quivered. "This trip, Casey and Monica, is particularly important to me. Let's not botch it up. Together, can we agree on that?"

"Yes, Mom. And a big bottle, or squeeze thing, or whatever you choose of ketchup. I'll be grilling burgers a bunch of times. Yes, they both like ketchup on their burgers. We should just assume," Tera said. She turned her head to the opposite side of the aisle, thumbed the ramen.

"Let's knock this out. You go on over and get eggs, bacon, and milk. And how about some yogurt for the mornings? We'll meet back in the snack aisle. I'll need help with that."

"Stick to the list, Mom. I'll also get butter, and the bread is over there, I think."

Tera left for the far side of the store, staring down at her cell phone, mumbling a bit about how she might get something different. Pauline nodded and thought to herself about what she usually does in these situations. From six up, that's when she knew, when she shook it off. 'Kids,' she would say. They're merely kids.

Pauline continued to pick at the condiments. Did anyone really like mustard? She looked down at the list. Tera would've put it on the list to appease anyone who might like mustard. She didn't think that anyone actually liked mustard. It just all seemed like so much to carry in. She might have to go off-list with Tera occupied elsewhere, make expert decisions.

Pauline saw Monica coming up the aisle and her breath stopped. An emptiness came over her chest and she gasped, glad to see her. Monica. She waved. Monica, with her store-standard grocery cart, kid seat down holding a few oranges and some celery, came up the aisle smiling as she careened.

Pauline noticed her blue horizontal striped shirt. It conjured images of Picasso or sailors. Monica probably thought sailors. Either way, she looked tidy, cute, and full of energy, ready for a trip.

"Pauline," Monica said. "It's so good to see you. We thought we might run into you here."

"It's so nice to get together finally."

Monica gleamed through the unsavory fluorescent light casting down on her. She gleamed gold through the jaundiced yellow hue of the fluorescent lights provided.

"Do we need mustard?" She broke into their smiling stares. "Does anyone really like mustard? I mean, in the world, really."

"You, you're absolutely right. No one should. I don't like mustard and Casey hates it. You're free to cross it off the list."

"That's so great. Done. And you have a list too? What do you have?"

"Staples. This and that. Frozen meat mostly. It's a brief list, really."

"Monica, I'm so glad we get along." Pauline almost broke down. Wetness formed in her eyes. "It's more than anything for the girls that we get along."

"Of course. I mean, a higher power destined the girls for each other. We aren't." She chuckled a bit and Pauline followed suit. "But it helps. I imagine joint vacations every year, but that's fine with me. I love to travel. And the girls are so great together."

"Yes, absolutely. Travel is so great, so this must be our best effort to get along." Pauline lowered her head and spoke the last words in a low tone, showing humor and also pointed seriousness. She wanted so much for the family to be good together. Pauline, herself, tried so hard.

After Pauline put the mustard back, they moved up the aisle, slowly but ready to part at the end. They, after all, had their own lists. Monica gripped the cart with a tension that showed she was still nervous. At the restaurant, her nervousness grew, Pauline thought. She ate her cake but was slow and intentional about it. She focused on keeping the fork still, resting it in her hand in between bites. Pauline had put hers down as she had learned from her mother so many years ago.

Monica wore a summer dress. She almost overdressed for the grocery store. Pauline wore a fashionable short-sleeved sweater and jeans. Monica's stiff dress stuck to her curves. It gave her a new shape over the existing. A little bigger than Pauline, both in height and figure, she still carried herself quickly and gently through a space. The dress had a decorative pattern of little purple flowers, but when one stepped back, it was almost geometric. She waved.

Pauline's mother died years ago. She called her every day, something Tera would never do, she thought. She was without genuine friendship with her daughter. They didn't have the same devotion she and her mother had had. That's what she thought, at least.

When they got to the end of the aisle, they moved to the part to go their separate ways. Pauline thought for a minute that Monica could be that for her, someone she called every day. A best friend. She couldn't pledge that it would all work out. But the absence in her life was something else. What if the girls got into a big fight? Would they also then not talk? Monica and Pauline's future would soon be told. Pauline wanted it to work, wanted at least this weekend to work.

They both glanced to the right at the top of the aisle, at the back of the store. The girls were mingling around the eggs, talking, leaning in, giggling. They were both happy to be together. It seemed their bliss carried through the entire grocery store, affected Monica and Pauline at that moment even. They were truly in love. Pauline thought for a moment.

She could hear them down the aisle. "Oh, stop." Casey pushed her shoulder into the stiff and sturdy Tera. Tera cradled the baby egg in her hands, happy to elbow Casey on each swing back and forth. Forth into Casey's side. She might hint at something, Pauline guessed.

"When would the two have children? When would it be time?" Pauline hoped she was not too old, was not past the age when children can sleep at Grandma's house and she could kneel on the floor to play games, show them the games of her mother's and her own childhood. Her stomach gave a strange contraction, and she thought, for a second, she herself might be pregnant. Lesbians have children later, she reminded herself. Perhaps that wasn't always true.

She would never have another child; she had chided aloud to Casey. Casey sighed and said neither would she. They both hoped in the quiet, or rather at least Pauline, that the girls would get along, have a wonderful trip, get married, have children. All in one thought, they more or less prayed it would happen.

Realizing their quiet, their spying on the girls, Pauline and Monica sped off in opposite directions. They would find their own worlds again. Those that were different alone with their daughters as a family from the world, they mashed together and created the new family. Each having loyalty but not taking sides.

At the registers, the mother daughter teams waved at each other and left out of opposite sides of the store. They hadn't even parked on the same side. Each had their own routine.

Pauline mused that she and Monica probably had brushed by each other before, and they had thought little of it. They were two different women with their own agendas and lives. They might not have ever intermingled if it wasn't for their daughters. But now they were a part of each other, bound, not by law yet, but by emotion, the emotion of others, their daughters.

Monica's snarky laugh and questioning looks lightened the mood every time. Her cartoonish giggle made everyone smile. The pair could be quick friends. They could survive stuck in a broken-down car together or stuck in an airport. Monica opened up about life and asked questions in the same turn. She prepared for the conversations and the talk flowed casually, freely. Friendship always followed if these key details presented themselves. And they already had it after a few interactions, one meeting about the girls.

Pauline hadn't ever had friendship at first sight, but if this was it, she was moving in full steam. She still needed to be sold on the idea. She and Monica were so different superficially, but their conversation, their intuition about each other, was strong and captivating. Monica seeped pride, calling

Monica her daughter's girlfriend's mom, and that's all that mattered. How could she be so lucky? There were no words.

Most in-laws were bound for tragedy. The two moms got along. They might never meet alone again, but they hit it off. That first step meant everything. They might just survive this cockamamy idea for a trip that Tera had concocted, planned so hard for, and wanted so much to work.

CHAPTER 7

The next day, Pauline was off to meet her old friend. She walked briskly through Main Street. She had parked her car some distance away from the restaurant, knowing she wouldn't be running errands or taking anything back with her. The walk from the car saved her some charges to her debit card, but that was not the reason she put the car where she did. She needed to clear her head.

Pauline set up a date with Samantha to relay the results of her visit to Robert, where she told him he was not to contact Samantha ever again. Robert considered himself a best friend. That's all she cared to say, enough to leave her guilt stricken.

She crept up the steps to the door of the brick row home. She was nervous as she always was with Samantha. Samantha had a certain power over her, that certain something that made her cower, and Pauline always asked for more.

Samantha blazed feisty eyes and twinkled her nose in a fluster when she didn't understand. She had always been rough and tumble to a degree. She loved to hike and exercise. She was the opposite of Pauline in many ways; but weren't so many of Pauline's friends really opposites? Didn't she yearn to see other lives? Samantha cleaned up nicely and mingled in the same circles as Pauline on the rare occasions she put on a dress.

Pauline didn't understand the reasoning. When Robert left, did he do it of his own accord? Was he mimicking Samantha, or had Samantha pushed him over the edge? Had Samantha, in fact, started the break-up? Regardless, the issue always moved back to the idea that Robert had started it all. Robert had made the issue begin. His departure had sprung everything into action. That had spurned his mid-life crisis and his foray into cooking. He had uniformly rejected his wife, and that was what left Samantha with scars.

Pauline mostly knew men to be the bad guys. There was her ex-husband who messed with her mind. She often thought about how lucky the girls were who got hit. It gave the indication to others that something was terribly wrong. It was a sign for them to step in. She knew it could be so much worse than what she got. She got the gaslighting and the abandonment. He would come home and criticize everything she did. It was always an endless weekend of: "the dishes have spots; you make a horrible meatloaf; and you have never cleaned the windows, ever."

He raised hands often as if he was going to hit, but he never let down the blow. Still, Pauline cowered in the home and even when he lifted his words at her in public. She never scared her. Never once somewhere visible.

She was glad when he left, but he kept coming back, flirting with her, toying with her emotions, making promises. For months, then years, she would've taken him back in a heartbeat. As he said, to bring up their daughter together. Pauline agreed. Then there were the presents, the very convertible she had to this day, given only several years ago. It was one last pity present, and Pauline knew it. He was working his magic, making her loyal, paying her off. And she knew it.

Still, Pauline thought Samantha needed to let it go. Let one instance go. She held on to the inciting incident, as well as the fact that when in Italy, Robert could have cheated. Those were the keywords she always used, "could have." She might've been rejecting the possibility for her own self-esteem, but it was true he might not have actually cheated.

Here she was now, with a lesbian, no less. And Pauline couldn't entirely wrap the change around her head. She understood that sometimes there is a point in your life when your body needs something different. New year for a new life. It wasn't her intention, her mind, to devastate Robert. Although that's how it happened. And it likely was the impetus for Robert's insistence on taking him back.

She walked by several shops she wished she had time to go

into, but she didn't. She and Monica and the girls were leaving sharply at 4:00 p.m. They had each taken some time off work and no one was going to tell them they wouldn't get out the door at 4:10 p.m. sharp. Monica had taken the entire day off, likely mostly because she was afraid of the wrath of the girls.

The shops were average sized and held average things, clothes, a place for knickknacks, a jewelry store. For a second, she paused. Should she get Monica a gift? A bracelet, not too fine, or a tchotchke? Then took back off on her way. She decided Monica would probably not do the same. Oh, how she liked to give gifts, though.

She was in Samantha's and Robert's, or just Samantha's now, larger than average main street sort of town, two clusters down from her own smaller than average city. Robert worked hard on his next food creation. Here was Pauline backstabbing, two faced, as usual to get some gossip.

Pauline was retired and nothing appeased her more than a good gossip session. This wouldn't be that. Samantha would likely be in tears or moaning about how she missed Robert. In a few minutes, she would get the complete story.

Pauline retired early some years ago after she split with her husband, taking a big lump sum of cash, the house, and the rental property. The summer house sold right away. She left him with their savings and the cars, and some artwork of decent value. Pauline could want nothing more than to get back to work. She needed to keep occupied, but couldn't find a hobby that gave structure, regularity. Often, she gauged she was going a little off-base and needed an exact time to get up, somewhere to be, to give her sanity. Next week, she was interviewing for a flower shop job, even though she had to decide whether to go on social security soon.

She stopped at the café, crawling with cats. They had taken over the convex exterior picture window. The grid work of silver painted muntin, some of the paint spilling over to glass, made the thing look like a submarine window of some sort. The cats all crawled into the interior of the submersible vessel.

Samantha was sitting on a seat, barely inside the ledge of the picture window. Pauline could see her before she entered. She already took short, almost faux sips from a proper coffee mug.

"Hi, Samantha."

"Oh, hello. I'm sorry I ordered." She pushed a mug of coffee with cream toward her. "No sugar, right?"

"Oh yes, that's it. Milk chocolate hue. This is great. Thank you."

"Two pieces of cheesecake in a bit?"

"Yes. That would be great." Pauline wavered a bit because it reminded her of her last slice of cake with Robert, or rather with Robert in the other room. Both loved desserts. Pauline imagined they had it every night when they were together.

"How are you?" Samantha said. "What have you been up to?"

"Oh, you know Tera and her girlfriend and her girlfriend's mom, Monica, and I are going on a trip. I am, I am super nervous. You know about Tera's anxiety. It's too much sometimes. Everything has to be perfect. It's horrible. She can't relax."

"I'm sure it'll be fine," Samantha said. "It can be a trial, right? A test of how much you can handle. Christmas will be a piece of cake after this."

"I'm not so sure Tera is sold on this one, but they are very much in love. They're always nuzzling up to each other. PDA is an issue. Let's simply say that," Pauline said.

Samantha seemed eager to talk, so Pauline dropped it and asked. "How are you?"

"She's really so great, Pauline." Samantha was giddy; the opposite of what Pauline would have expected.

Samantha disregarded Robert, Pauline's close friendship with Robert. Samantha should have at least feigned some despair.

"She's sweet and sensitive. And her touch."

It appalled Pauline. "Oh, that sounds nice."

Pauline had gone online and met someone herself, Cathy. Maybe that was her bite of anger, her jealousy. She was poking around doing research on the internet, looking for details on women. For Robert, she told herself. She combed through dictionaries and Human Rights Council links. She re-learned about her body parts from AutoStraddle. Whatever did that name mean?

Eventually, she signed up for a dating app to meet someone. Just to talk. She wanted to have a conversation about what drives lesbians, essentially get to the bottom of why had Samantha not known. Why had she done this to Robert?

Cathy was so nice. Sometimes offended, she countered with non-answers. Others were compassionate, compelling, and inviting. She wanted Pauline to be satisfied with herself. She came on to Pauline. Pauline liked it.

"She's just." The words spit out rather quickly. "She's so much better than Robert. Flowers aside. She's given me so much. I mean, Robert gave me flowers, but so did Mar, and she left notes with them. It's a small thing, but it meant so much. They are in a box. A box I haven't put things in since high school. It's like I'm alive again. Mar, she's just the world. She asks me how I'm doing, invites me to sit down after work and talk about how my day was, what was bad even. She wants me to feel free to complain, and she even rubs my feet."

Pauline watched Samantha look down at her freshly cut fingernails and Pauline guessed what came next. Only Samantha didn't say it, she didn't say 'The sex is great.' She didn't go that far.

Pauline could only imagine. She wanted to find out what sex with a woman amounted to in bed. Pauline really dove deep with Cathy. Even so, something lacked some sincerity. She couldn't fully imagine what the sex was like. She wouldn't know what to do. "I probably never will." Pauline almost mumbled it aloud. She was jealous.

The cheesecake came out, and they took small bites, looking each other in the eyes. Samantha had a wide smile; one you could get right after sex. One with satisfaction, almost glee. Pauline's smile was inward, devilish at most. She lingered on thoughts of her own Cathy and masked the emotion while eyeing Samantha back.

"So, it's over? I am kind of here on behalf of Robert." She chewed nonchalantly, almost bitterly, in the name of Robert. Pauline gave the sobering reality. It took Samantha aback, and she realized just then that she and Samantha weren't so close. They hadn't so much in common. Pauline leaned toward Team Robert, despite how they'd gotten to know each other recently. Despite that, Pauline, a woman herself, might understand her passion for another woman. Unbeknownst to Samantha, Pauline kind of did.

"We've been over this," Samantha said. "He can't keep coming back and asking. I thought he got it when I sent you last week."

Samantha continued on, "It's so much, really. I mean, we've been at it, working on a relationship for four years. Four years of breakups and reconnects after ten years of a good solid honeymoon relationship. Honestly, though, it really cannot work. We cannot keep going back and starting over. It's just not starting over at this point. I just really need to never talk to him again. For the life of God, I never want to see him ever again. I need to move on with that pain, with that rollercoaster of emotions. It's entirely different and entirely the same as I hear it."

"The worst was my ex. Custody talks, and that's it. It was never—"

"I thought he got it at dinner when we didn't talk. You left early, but we really didn't have a word with each other," Samantha said, cutting Pauline off.

"Because I crushed his soul a few hours before," Pauline said. "I had to do it, but I didn't like it."

"Do you have bitterness toward me, Pauline, because I could never—"

"No. I understand Robert's emotion as if he were here with us now. It's so tough being caught in the middle of this. You deserve your happiness—"

A cat jumped on Pauline's lap and a few pieces of fur flew and then floated in the air close to the last bites of cake. "A cat café. Such a tough place to eat," Pauline said. It really was a wonderful place for two people to meet that didn't want to go too deep. You could always get distracted, look the other way toward a cat and change the topic in a flash.

His tag said muffins. Pauline flipped it over a few times in her hands.

"Maybe Robert would want a cat?"

"That's too much Samantha. You truly are happy, but I can't. Robert will be fine. I'll confirm with him. I just…It's hurting me too, going back and forth between you both." Pauline resolved not to act as a go between anymore. She was going on vacation. If it started up again, if Robert started calling Samantha again, so be it. She would not be getting involved.

"I must take a break from you both. I'll call one or the other in two months. You all have to work this out yourself."

"Oh, Pauline. Don't leave like this," Samantha said.

"I've got to go get my luggage. The girls and Tera's girl-friend's mom and I are going on vacation. So, I won't be able to help you see." Pauline lingered with her jacket in her hands. She stepped into it after a pause. She wanted to leave on a friendly note, but this would suffice.

"Dear Pauline. We'll talk again, right?"

"Oh, course we will." Another cat skirted past Pauline as she shuffled out the door.

She dashed back toward the car. It was 1:00 p.m. and she could not, for several reasons, be late. The girls would murder her, for example. Her sanity would be compromised on the trip if the girls were upset. If she arrived late, she would be the primary cause of the turmoil.

The car sat vacant in the disheveled and overgrowing lot. Not broken into. No ticket. She had lucked out and would enjoy the extra four dollars. In fact, she talked for over an hour with Samantha, so she would've gotten a ticket. She did the math in her head.

CHAPTER 8

Tera and Casey had taken the day off even though they weren't leaving for the rental until much later. They had come to an understanding. This would be a wonderful vacation. Tera was adamant, and Casey followed suit.

The morning had rolled over, but that didn't stop Tera from going for a run. She was a plain clothes soldier. She burned off stress.

Sweat trickled down Tera's face as she sprinted and relaxed to a slower run, sprinted and relaxed. A benefit run took place in one month, and she wanted to be prepared. After two more races this summer, and possibly not until next year because she'd have to register and swim train, she'd take a shot at triathlons.

She headed down the street of her suburban neighborhood. Most of the houses were like-minded, built together a few decades ago. "This would be the place she would also graduate into," she thought with a bit of a sour face. The property owners cut the house they lived in into three apartments. An anomaly in an otherwise modernly developed neighborhood, their house boasted four stories. Its huge Victorian presence could easily be converted into a bed-and-breakfast with frequent rental matching the amount brought in from renters, if not more. They were close to a college and would get mild mannered parents and visiting students. It rested at the corner of the developed neighborhood like a gate or entryway.

She wanted a picket fence and wasn't sure if the need would fade. Now she had to settle in. She agreed with her mom when she said it; she wanted control and to have stability. And that wasn't a terrible thing in her mind. She wanted to see two kids and a dog, at least four bedrooms, with one for her mom to stay over. Her mom wanted that. She was sure: two children and a big house, likely not the white picket fence.

Surely, she was being dated. She didn't want the apron, the apple pie, to stand like the rest of them. It could've been an internalized homophobia that was causing her to want to be like everyone else, not be unique, to celebrate her community. She forgave herself.

Things happened behind closed doors. She wouldn't find peace in this environment. Dysfunctional families flourished in neighborhoods like these. Heads of household battered women. Children lashed out or ran away. People fell into debt. It was all the same, but again, hidden, no one could see. Everyone was full of lies you told people every day.

Her own family became dysfunctional like this. Her father left them to cavort with younger women, party at the beach, drive fast cars. A monster in plain sight, his spirit remained even after he left.

She would find Casey in her life. However, she persisted in her pursuit of finding a house, a place that resembled status and gain, stability. They had grown close and while Casey might not be in that last place to settle down into a house with a white picket fence, Tera knew she would always be a part of her life. She would always ask her questions about her style if it was good enough, appropriate, hot. Tera would always check in because she wanted to know what Casey might be doing. She needed to believe that Casey would still love her.

When Tera came back from her morning run, which actually started a little later in the afternoon, she moved right up to the bedroom to take a shower and gather her belongings.

"I packed already. I'm taking a shower and we'll be ready to go." Tera seeped sass. The moms wouldn't be there for several hours.

Casey sprawled out on the bed, hoping to get some affection. Somehow, she understood now was not the time.

"Don't you ever lose control? Her body splayed across the entire bed."

"No. Not really. I try to keep things where they should be." Tera moved an errant sock back to its drawer but didn't search for its companion.

"Tera. Really. You'd miss this." Casey got what she was saying.

Tera pulled around to the opposite side of the bed and gave Casey a kiss. She pulled her shirt off, throwing it toward her head as she made her way to the shower.

Casey followed, grabbing Tera by the hands behind her back and waiting swimmingly as the steam from the shower became hotter and hotter.

Casey found Tera's hips before she could find the strength in the steam, after the exhausting run, to lower her shorts. She pushed her back against the wall and lifted her foot, pulling sock, then sock, shorts, then boy shorts. Tera raised her shirt only to have Casey pull it clean off. Tera wrangled the sports bra over her head and wiped the dewy sweat from her forehead.

Lathering was a game, and they found the details of the other's bodies in the areas dealt with through a cursory overview when they showered by themselves. They were kissing behind the ears, and at the small of the back, hips thrust in.

Their wetness mingled with wetness, mingled with steam, and soaped up sweat. They were together in a unison of the same warmth, sharing their bodies with each other and melding.

"I love this and you," Tera said the words earnestly. She loved Tera and would love her forever and ever. Casey might not be the last one for Tera to love. But the words came out easily because they were true.

"Let's skip out and leave the moms. You and me." Casey pulled her head back and winked with her right eye.

"Absolutely," Tera said.

And they collapsed back into each other as Casey swam on Tera's neck and Tera dug into more precious parts. They co-mingled, trying to find each other's new sweet spot. Only they knew them all so well. Casey came when she was told.

When Tera's fingers reach the extent of her pleasure. She subsided in Tera's arms until Tera begged for her own moment, already taken with the steam, and the sweat, and the crush of Casey's final climaxing moans.

Cascading her arms around Tera's body: head, to neck, to breasts, and hips, Casey tried to tease her to even deeper moans. Tera was willing to find only one point, and begged ever so softly into Casey's ear, "Please."

Casey gently slipped herself into Tera's want and her moans flipped to coarse, high-pitched exertions of joy with each thrust. Tera found herself fully morphed under Casey's doing, and her adoration exploded into a final exertion. When they both collapsed, this time Casey on top of Tera against the side of the shower, and with Tera enjoying Casey's full weight, they felt calmed, relaxed, without bitterness or anger.

As they got dressed, tensions rose slightly. They were now behind schedule, per Tera's watch. The couple rushed to dry and still damp, put on fresh clothes. They smelled spectacular, but their hair was wet. "Would someone notice their afternoon delight?" Tera thought.

Each of the two girls carried their own suitcases, as well as an extra bag, all at once. Somehow, it would all fit in the car. The trip ahead of them, the journey with two moms, would be a test of their relationships, compatibility, and patience. The relationships, Tera's and Casey's, and the bonds between the daughter and the mother, besides the new mom friendship, would require a certain sensitivity and finesse. For them all to get along would be an absolute miracle.

"Did you remember your toothbrush?" Tera said.

"Yes," Casey said.

"The brush?"

"Yup."

"Extra shampoo? Just take what we have in the shower."

"Yes. Yes. Yes. Except the shampoo. I checked and they have it there."

"But honey. It's probably cheap stuff. I mean, wouldn't it

be better to have our stuff that we usually have? Cheap shampoo makes my hair frizzy."

The two pushed forward, gathering things from the kitchen and the basement.

"Bring up some paper towels." Tera shouted from the top of the stairs.

They bumbled down the steps toward the front door, then Tera, off balance, dropped all her luggage at the entrance. Casey nearly slammed into her and, heels breaking, she dropped her bags as well.

"Oh God." Casey sucked in and held a breath tightly, puffing out her chest as if there was going to be a fight.

"I, it's that." Tera had stress lines on her forehead. "I simply want to make sure this all goes well. You know?"

"Of course it will. Straighten up darling. It will all be fine. If we have to go to a drugstore to get shampoo, so be it," Casey said.

Tera's mom had made her make lists as a child for when they traveled. Every time they would go somewhere, out would come that same list. Wrinkled and chewed, torn with food on it by the time she was twelve, the list always came with them. That list likely persisted still. She could find it tucked away in a drawer somewhere in her mom's house, moved when she moved out on Tera's dad hidden in a crevasse with high school report cards and a handprint from kindergarten.

Other things likely lie hidden too. Pictures of her first girlfriend, tenth grade, a remnant of a prom date, a guy, unbelievably, posters from her dorm room wall. These things may or may not have been combined in that one memory drawer her mother had. These things, her personal items, were somewhere. They'd just as soon be kept safe with the rest, but Tera would have to find them. She wasn't quite at that age yet, her thirties or forties, when she'd need to look back, obsessively search to find the things she hid when embarrassment was the predominant emotion. Those things existed. She was certain. Without her mom's oversight, though, she just didn't understand where.

Tera descended into the basement to gather up some paper products. Apparently, she had forgotten napkins, paper towels, plates, and plastic silverware. Casey had told Tera she didn't need any of it, yet Tera headed directly to the basement, and with a solid "Ugh," gathered the things.

The basement was musty and filled with old boxes, piles of memories that belonged to the owner. She wanted none of it. She didn't want the stuffed rabbit that crept out of the side of a box or the rocking chair in the corner. It all became creepy, like a scary movie in an instant.

She didn't keep any of her own boxes at her mom's house. They had dispersed things: mix tapes to the garbage, school report cards to the trash, and love notes burned in a fire. This all occurred when her mom and her dad got a divorce when Tera was fifteen. She never accumulated much after that because she always imagined she'd have to clean it all out, dispose of it, like she did that summer when her dad left, and they moved from an almost mansion into a two-bedroom apartment just by her school.

Tera's dad was a deadbeat, and he hadn't wanted to pay support at first or sign divorce papers that aligned with Tera's mom's expectations. Tera hated him even when she traveled to Florida in the summers. She was pro-Pauline for at least two years. Everything Pauline did, she stuck to her. Everything she said, Tera believed. But when she was a teenager, she rejected Pauline so much more. She called it for what it was.

Tera disowned her father. The moment he left. She assigned it the word hatred, and it brewed inside of her. The sentiments came out sometimes, and the anger came out at other times. They were not always related.

She got into fights, and counselors talked to her at school because of the "raging anger" she exhibited throughout the day. It was truly a problem for a while. But she outgrew it. Or so she thought, at least. She rarely acted out and stayed tame and in place when confronted with biting comments. That's what Tera thought about herself. But she recognized the trauma, the deep imbedded anger that her father's departure had put there. And with the help of the school's counselor, she knew that her brain processed these emotions unbeknownst to her and they could erupt. She must be vigilant. She must take care. And she thought she did, mostly.

"Your mom will be here any minute." Casey yelled down from the top of the stairs again. She hadn't moved, almost pausing, waiting for a response to her request for paper towels.

The steps creaked as Tera ascended. She slipped on the steps with all the things in her hand. She was rushing as usual and could have cascaded down the stairs to her doom, become just another memory. Casey didn't see.

"I don't think these are even ours. They might be from the last renters or the basement tenants."

Casey asked where to take the bags that were blocking the front door. The moms wouldn't be able to get in.

"Just put stuff in the driveway," Tera said.

Tera moved to remove a smudge from Casey's forehead, and Casey leaned in, smiling.

They embraced and Casey's head moved deep past Tera's and then turned to her ear, quietly speaking in almost a whisper. "It's going to be okay. We will get through this."

Staring straight ahead, Tera said, "I didn't think this would happen. It will be a miracle if we make it out alive, if they live to tell tales." Tera's face turned pouty as she mimed unhappiness.

With a screech of the wheels, a car pulled into the driveway. This was to be a trip of all trips, a family memory none of them would forget. Pauline was taking control of the wheel of a red convertible. It would be a tight fit for all four passengers with limited leg room and small seats, but it was worth it. It had a convertible top.

Casey wielding bags moved to the deep red convertible. It was shinier than anything she had ever seen. Top down, Tera's mom prepared for business. She portrayed herself always more or less at the ready, whether it was for a game of trivia or scrabble, a healthy political debate, or a book club chat. Her competitive streak always came through. Pauline, what Casey called her, didn't get out of the car.

"Top up or down."

"Up—" Casey said

"Definitely up, Mom," Tera said. "Let's ease into this." She whispered the words in Casey's ear. "No one can hear well with the top down."

"Cops are twice as likely to pull over a red car?" Pauline said. "What do the kids say, Tera? You only live once. YOLO." She tilted her head back and coughed out a laugh.

Casey giggled with pleasure.

Tera looked Casey in the eyes. With intentional movement, she rolled them almost across her brow.

Monica pulled up to the house a few minutes later, as the last of the grocery bags full of nonperishables and paper products, coffee and filters went into the trunk. Tera and Casey stepped back in wonder that it all fit. A few items would go between Casey and Monica in the back.

"Monica," Pauline said. "It's so nice to meet you." Pauline extended her hand, and Monica took it in her own loosely. They exchanged smiles.

The two grown women mouthed some laughs while the girls looked on blankly, unaffected, and Monica leaned over the driver's side door to hug Pauline. This would be the trip.

"You too, uh, know each other," Tera said. "Remember? You met a month ago at that potluck?"

"Oh, darling. We were teasing." Pauline reached out to touch Tera and then at once turned and muddled about arranging luggage as if to change the subject entirely.

Monica threw a glare at Pauline. Pauline smiled broadly and evenly, without tension, and unstressed.

CHAPTER 9

"This weather is marvelous." Pauline joked, articulating the words with her lips. It didn't resonate. She smoothed her slacks on her thighs in response, brushing her hands together moments later.

Tera set down two suitcases outside the front door and turned to lock the house. They would be gone for seven days. The trunk was open. Her mom had popped it upon arrival. The girls could load swiftly, and they would all get the journey started. Tera clunked the two suitcases down the steps. The weight was too much for her and after dropping one on a step below her; she fell downward and lost her balance. She recovered; she was a bit embarrassed but smiling.

"Oh boy. Mom. Your hair. It's going to be a mess after five minutes let alone the hours it will take to get us to the lakes," Tera said.

"It's okay. Really. You are certainly the only thing I care about right now. It's great to be with you all. Let's set the hair issue aside and enjoy what is going well, our conversation and company. Right?"

"Yes. Of course, Mom. It'll be marvelous either way," Tera said.

They sidled into their seats, and Pauline revved the engine for effect. This was it, the trip of the year. Their lives and relationships depended on it.

They took off, hair flying. Monica tried to talk but as she did, Tera watched wisps of hair whip into her mouth and soon she spat and picked at it, trying to get it out of her teeth. She lashed out with words but said little.

As the wind funneled into her right ear, Tera couldn't hear well. She could hear someone say something and then a rush of wind would dampen all the excitement, or it left her wondering what the joke had been. Tera scratched at her head, wondering when to intervene and tell her mom to pull over.

Tera's mom herself must've seen a need. Even with the windshield breaking some of the noise and frustrating winds, she wasn't immune to the disaster in the convertible. Tera noticed her mom asked Monica two, then three questions with no answers. She simply shrugged and carried on. Something eventually must've clicked.

Ten minutes later, they were off the road at an emergency stop off.

"I'm so sorry. I can't. It really will be a wreck," Monica said. Her hands feverishly pulled at clumps of hair knotted and stringy, while Tera and Casey struggled to get the top up. Tera's mom stayed put in the front driver's seat applying another coat of lipstick in the rearview mirror.

The second sendoff was much better, and the group piped up with conversation. There were questions and responses. Monica's words followed Tera's mom's as much as Casey's. Tera interjected with bits of conversation and facts almost on cue. Worry plagued her, that things might not pan out. Her mom would lose her temper, Casey's mom her patience.

The exhaust fumes no longer wafting in and out of the back seat, everyone was free to speak about what was on their mind.

Conversation flowed from what everyone did that day to the past week. Monica and Casey chatted in the back about an issue she was having at work. Everyone was having an enjoyable time. The friendships and bonding grew right in front of Tera. Everyone appeared as if they would rather be nowhere else.

They talked about the agenda and what their favorite wineries were based on internet research. Everyone had a comment about which was the best graphic for the particular set of wineries. Casey leaned over everyone to show a picture of a winery with Celtic knots and cats. Everyone craned their necks to see. Tera's mom even ran over the center line of the road trying to look.

It wasn't until someone brought up the gay agenda that the talk turned to sexuality and gender.

"The gay agenda? What's that? Like all the gay wineries you want to go to?" Monica asked with a chuckle.

"Yeah. Kind of, Mom. It's an obligation," Casey said.

"Count me in." Monica bit back.

Sex was a difficult topic for Tera and Casey's parents. But Casey's mom had questions, and she wasn't afraid to ask them at this venue. She dove right in at the beginning of the trip, into a topic any mom of a lesbian daughter thinks about constantly: what do all these words mean?

"I just don't understand all the terms," Casey's mom said.

"Mom, you need to join PFLAG or something. There are so many resources out there, do some research," Casey said.

"Right, and these abbreviations. Duh, I should just get it," Casey's mom quipped.

"No. It's okay, Monica. I tried to do research. Not only do you have to worry about gay men greased up…" Monica paused, "Not that it is so bad. But you have to commit to learning a new language, trying to understand AutoStraddle and all these weird rants that don't really seem to make sense. It's difficult because the lingo is knee deep, and me, as a straight person, I really need an interpreter."

"Ok. I see. Mom, you don't have to follow AutoStraddle. I'm sorry Mom that I jumped at you. It's just…"

"Pansexual. What's that?" It was two hours in, and they still had a few hours to go.

"A pansexual is someone who identifies as having attraction to people regardless of gender," Tera said.

"Attraction, Tera, attraction. That's the real crux of it. The attraction can be emotional or romantic. There are many shades."

The car fell silent, and everyone stared straight ahead as if the radio said someone shot Kennedy. Both girls felt their moms were on a constant journey to catch up, belong to the LGBTQ+ community. A difficult topic to broach for a straight woman in late mid-life, they were constantly learning, constantly asking questions. And that, if nothing else, was good. Their journey began, in the same measure, to learn more about each of the four of them. They all claimed liberty to be open.

"All I know," Monica said. "Is that when you were ten, you told me you didn't like dolls, and you did like softball, and you didn't like boys the way girls were supposed to like boys?" Monica took a deep breath. "And then you told me you knew what that meant. We both knew what that meant." Monica dipped her head and brushed away a tear forming in the corner of her eye. "And that's all I needed to know to love you, and I still love you that way. The mail person doesn't deliver Out Magazine to our house anymore…and I sneaked a peak…but I know I love you and that's all that matters."

They all smiled in silence this time. Monica dipped her head a few times more, using the back of her hand on the corners of her eyes. No one could top Monica's proclamation of her love for her lesbian daughter.

"That didn't stop Nickey from chasing me around all day and knuckling me in the head every time he caught up," Casey said.

"Who's Nickey?" Pauline asked.

"Ugh. Her cousin," Monica said. "He told her it was to make her faster for softball."

"Mom, he yelled in my ear, 'You better turn out straight,' every time," Casey said.

Pauline piped up. "My daughter came out when she was sixteen. And we fought and fought. But that doesn't mean I don't love her to this day." Pauline looked into the rearview mirror at Monica and winked.

Besides some carrying on and bickering, they were all enjoying themselves thoroughly. Pauline called the back and forth between Tera and Casey to a stop several times with a blunt, "Girls."

Casey broke down several times. "Tera, stop looking at your phone."

Pauline sternly said, "Girls." Tera's rebuttal was no match.

Things fell silent for another fifteen miles until they all forgot about the incident.

The carousing started with Pauline, out of character. She piped up and sang a Fleetwood Mac song. All four of them joined in for what seemed like hours. Casey's mom interrupted, only to debate that Christine McVie was the best singer. Tera's mom flat out told her to shut up and say it wasn't true. They all scurried back to their corners. Casey's mom's head lingered on the door next to the window as she hummed quietly to herself, defeated but knowing all too well which singer was her favorite.

Monica bopped her head from side to side. Casey swayed. But Tera and her mom both belted out the lyrics, emoting with their necks and chins on the key words, over singing, performing, performing.

"What are your hopes and dreams, Mom?" Tera said.

"That's a random question. Did you get it out of a book?" Casey asked.

"Well, yeah." As she responded, her voice rose. "I mean, how else are we to figure out what to talk about? For open communication," Tera said. "My mom always used to ask this question. To like everyone."

"Well, I think we're doing pretty well," Casey's mom said.

"Hopes and Dreams." Tera's mom tapped her upper lip with her index finger. "I guess. Well recently, I always wanted to go to Maine. I guess I could find love there, you know."

"Strange you never mentioned Maine before."

"Yup. My most recent hope and dream…Check out Maine."

"I think you should go for it. As soon as you have the chance." Tera nodded with her support.

Tera piped up, disrupting her own conversation that started, that didn't seem to end. "The gas station is right up here."

"Serendipity. I must stretch my legs," Tera's mom said.

"Blame the powers that be," Tera said. "You know that…"

When they got to the gas station, which Tera had planned

out as a specific stop on the way, Casey's mom burst out of the car door. Her butt tensed and legs shuffled toward the restroom in the station's rear.

Tera's mom jumped up and out too, leaving Tera to empty the trash from all the various nooks and crannies. Casey would pump gas. Soon after, Tera followed her mom, ringing a jingling bell as she entered the store once Casey got to work. Tera's mom had been moseying around the store, looking for the perfect munchies. Touching candy bar after candy bar, it seemed she couldn't find the perfect one. Tera tackled the chip aisle, knowing full well her mom would never choose a candy bar. They screamed too many calories. It had always been that way. Her mom was out of the corner of her vision the whole time.

Someone smacked something metal loudly on the counter.

"Ok. Everybody down." A gun shot up glistening at the top of a raised arm. He shook his wrist left and right and the gun appeared loose in his grasp. "I don't want to fire this."

Tera questioned whether he ever had as her head darted to the car, where Casey was mulling about, squeegeeing the windows. Tera dropped to the floor.

"Ok. Everybody. Nobody gets hurt. Let's all work on that. Stay still. Don't do anything your mom wouldn't do in this situation."

The cashier's register dinged as it opened, a lever on the bottom pulled without hesitation. "This is my fifth time. Look, I don't get paid enough. Take it."

The man in a black ski mask with a shiny silver gun raised in his right arm, now tired, and collapsed into his side, lunged at the register with his left arm.

"You're supposed to tell me to do that."

"No funny business. Put it in that bag, plastic."

The cashier abided and placed tens and twenties from the right in the bag, grabbing the ones and change last before pulling out several chunks of bills from under the tray.

The man continuously slammed his fist now on the

counter. Each time he did it, Tera's whole body jumped an inch off the ground. Her neck stiffened and she couldn't move if she wanted to. Her shoulders locked, and it was over.

He coughed a deep, hoarse cough. Tera could hear him struggling with the cashier, looking for more money or stifling him so he wouldn't press the robbery button.

A familiar jingle lit the air. A jingle that rang on millions of corner stores, gas stations, dry cleaners, and other behind the counter stores.

Everyone rested their elbows on the floor and lifted their heads. Tera's mom was okay. Some strange man she saw when she entered rose and moseyed up to the register to pay for his drink. He asked if this happened often. Tera thought it was a funny thing to ask, but did not listen to the answer.

Tera got up and hobbled over to her mom. She confirmed she was all right, holding her by the shoulders and almost shaking her while she tried to tame her own nerves. They watched Casey out the window with an open jaw trace the getaway car as it barreled down the road. Tera's mom pointed at her. "Casey duck."

"She's okay now. I'm sure. Monica is still in the bathroom."

Tera's mom paused, let out an exasperated, quiet grunt, and smoothed her pants before moving to the counter. "So, what do we do now?" Tera's mom asked the clerk.

"Hey, are you okay?" Tera interjected.

"Yeah. Fine, thanks," The clerk said. "And five times. This is my fifth. I get a raise every time. Not much, but you get it."

"So, if you're okay. We're going to go, I guess."

"Well, the cops come, and I guess you can stay, or you, if you can't, you can't. The other guy left. They'll probably want your statements. I need a witness."

Tera's mom stared at Tera and then said, "We have to scuttle. We're on vacation, you see, and there's no time." She shuffled toward the door.

"We're on vacation. Tell them that. Here I'll leave my number if they want to call. Sure is taking a bit."

"Yeah, they're out Old Mill Road. It'll be a half hour."

Tera slipped into the driver's seat as her mom was dawdling in the store talking to the clerk. She thought it was for the best because her mom still seemed dazed, talkative, and bubbly, but a little off. This was probably a normal reaction to events, but Tera wanted to relieve some extra pressure on her mom.

If the trip had six phases, they would be what are you doing, work, open communication, singing, hopes and dreams, and dead silence. No one said a word. When Casey's mom emerged from the women's restroom around the corner, she did not understand what had happened. She was in utter disbelief when they all bounded into the car, Casey's jaw still not back in place.

"It was a robbery. That simple. We survived," Tera said.

"They had guns? I thought I heard some shouting," Casey's mom said.

And there was quiet. Somehow, Casey's mom understood not to ask too many questions just yet. She dipped her head, and Tera could see her checking her phone, likely for new articles, accounts of similar robberies, the local police's website. The witnesses dealt with their limited trauma and the car continued to lurch forward to their destination.

Almost as if she didn't believe them, she scoured the internet. At one point, she held up her hand to Casey, who was asking her what would've happened if she came out into the mess. She shushed her daughter and torqued her head back to look at the internet.

That set the mood for the rest of the trip. No one said a word, until Pauline spoke up almost as if the whole things had never happened and said, "What's for dinner?"

"Salmon and potatoes," Casey said.

Pauline's grin did not dissipate, but it was as if there were no more words on earth, as if they had used them up. Pauline did not say another word. She did not change the mood if that was her intent. The event struck them all, and they used the time in silence, Monica on the internet. Casey furiously texted a friend. Tera looked at her mom every five seconds to see if she was okay. And Pauline, arms folded, sat idle as they down the highway smiled with a false grin. It appeared she was trying her hardest to wipe the emotion out of everyone's thoughts and actions, the things they had yet to say, so they could all relax and have an enjoyable time.

CHAPTER 10

In the car, the four of them leaned this way and that as they rounded corners on a surly street. They were getting closer. The GPS confirmed it, and all eyes were on the darn thing, watching Tera, now driving, make turns in real time. The tunes were slightly quieter now, and Tera could barely make out who she thought sounded like Def Leppard, even though she shimmied up to the speaker in the front seat. Someone had changed the channel, but she muted it just the same.

Tera slowed to almost a stop, looking for the right house. She entered a driveway, and several Dobermans came leaping at her. She spun in the arched driveway and immediately pointed her way out. It was a quick turnaround. The dogs clamored behind her, and she heard someone yell that they were going for a gun. Beads of sweat formed on Tera's forehead and her grip on the wheel tensed.

She popped over to the next driveway, guessing that it was the right place. Hoping. As they parked, the dogs ran up to them and were about to leap into the open roofed car, except a strong burdened voice called them back. "Dogs," the voice said. "Okay," Tera thought to herself. "This is not a neighborly place."

When the coast was clear, the four got out of the car, stepping gingerly on the crushed gravel dented here and there, not really serving its overall purpose.

At 9:30 p.m., they couldn't see much more clearly. The rough rancher of a house topped with a low-pitched roof looked kind of like a trailer from outside. Tera thought it might be a trailer because she had never been in one.

The bright orange door hit like it did in the rental photos. It gave the house character, an edgy appeal, but the stained siding just made it out to be what it was all over, a cheap place to crash. The rental company got her with the orange door.

"Well, this is just awful," Tera said. As she entered, she dragged her finger across the kitchen counter, and it left streaks of grease in its place. She took the other hand to the top of the microwave and dust spilled over the edge. "Thought so," Tera said as everyone else looked on.

"No, really. It's not that bad." Casey bit at her cuticles.

Tera sauntered over to the sink. "If the bathroom is as gunky as this faucet junction with the sink, we're all in trouble." She snarked, half joking, and coughed out a laugh.

"Oh. This is absolutely...not horrible." Monica's voice trailed off from down the hall.

Tera and Casey exchanged glances. They both knew it really was.

The furniture was minimal and sparse. None of the four kitchen table chairs matched. The wallpaper was peeling in the living room, but it actually appeared more pleasant to sit there than in the kitchen eating area, where there actually were chairs, because the cracks in the table made Tera think about life and death.

Tera roamed around the first floor, looking for a door to the basement. "This is no, no, no, not good." They had to keep the cleaning supplies somewhere.

Tera turned back to the sink, almost wallowing, and picked at the rusted red with a scouring sponge. She pulled back from the sink only when Casey rested her crossed arms on Tera's back. She moved to kiss her neck and then Tera turned back and held her, almost whimpering. "I just wanted it to be perfect."

"It's not always perfect. Right? That rental company is dicey. We always get a place with something," Casey said.

"Right." Tera rubbed a spot on the linoleum floor with the rubber toe of her shoe.

"Don't try. Don't ruin this. It will all be okay. You need to relax, fall into and deal with the unknown."

Tera's mom appeared in the doorway. "Really girls, Monica and I don't think it's that bad."

"Did you see the neighbors? Their Dobermans are barking at us. They'll bark all night, probably. They looked vicious when they penned them up. Like they'd ravage us if the neighbors let them back out again."

"Tera." Casey rested her head back on Tera's shoulder. "We're here together. You're spiraling. Just try."

"Really, Pauline and I are okay," Casey's mom said. "It'll be all right. What's on the agenda for tomorrow? Tera, now I get it. It has all been planned out."

"We thoroughly covered this, Mom. Wine tasting. With cheese. Ten spots."

Tera's mom clapped her hands, and a huge smile rose on her face. To Tera, she appeared to be a young child full of glee.

"I'm delighted. Oh, and Robert will be so jealous. He said to bring back only the absolute best." Tera's mom returned and clapped her hands again after she spoke. "Monica, this is so great."

Casey's mom wasn't so excited, but a big grin came across her face for Tera's mom. "Pauline, of course. We'll really get to know each other with what ten wineries planned?"

"Oh, I'll spill my guts Monica, I really will." Tera's mom grabbed Casey's mom by the arm and scurried her way toward the bedrooms. She picked up her bag and when they were all the way down the hall, she let go of Monica's arm and turned to enter the room she had picked for her own. It was the one less desirable, all things considered. "These girls are so on edge. I can't." They exchanged glances and Tera's mom popped her head out of the room to call to the daughters. "Girls." Tera's mom yelled from where she had settled in. "I'm going to relax and read. There's too much tension in the kitchen. Wake me up early, of course."

Tera could hear the bleeps from her mom's computer as it started up. The sound carried in the barely furnished, empty room.

In the middle of the night, Tera scurried out of the bedroom, leaving Casey behind snoring loud and clear. She shuffled her feet on the cold floor. Two holes in her socks caught on the tackiness of the linoleum. Tera could hear her mom talking on the phone to someone. She wasn't sure who it was or who it could be. She could hear a few loud whispers, and she seemed light and happy. Tera could tell that much. Her laughter bellowed out as loud as it could from someone stifling their every noise. It couldn't be Tera's father, that much she was sure of.

Tera's father left them both when Tera turned fifteen. As Tera reckoned, it was before he'd need to pay for her to go to some expensive private school. Tera was having trouble, but she was a teenager. Drama came with the age. They argued about the school, and Tera thought it was partially her fault. He ran off with a younger woman to Florida, leaving Tera and her mom to fend for themselves until the support checks could be determined. Tera's father made a lot of money, but it didn't make up for the, albeit lukewarm, love he gave them both for over fifteen years. He would say it was too far to travel to visit Tera. A few weeks a summer, he would organize for her to visit him. A few years, something came up and she never even made the trip. Those summers, she could hear her mother yelling on the phone ten times louder than she was at the moment. Tera rested on the steps, unable to come down and comfort her mom, who she found to hurt more than herself. She still dreamed about getting old and didn't linger on the past. Tera had forgotten about her father. Her mother had not.

As she stood in the hall, a matte black notebook caught her eye. She scurried into the kitchen quickly to open it. She snooped. Tera's mom had never been a journal writing person, so the book was intriguing. She filled it with notes about the trip. Things she wanted to see and do. Flipping to another tab labeled Maine, she found similar notes. The Scarborough Fair, the markets, "a mountain hike in crisp air." Pauline's mom had never hiked. She had never wanted to. This whole thing was odd. There were multiple notes, someone named Cathy. A phone number.

Tera's mom coughed loudly in the bedroom down the hall and Tera shut the notebook quickly, replacing a fabric bookmark likely in the wrong place. Her mom chased the cough with some more whispered laughter.

She filled a glass quietly and sipped at it over the sink. The glasses had detergent spots and somehow it comforted her. Someone had washed them. Her mom had never been secretive. She had always shared. Or maybe it had been that Tera always shared. Pauline interjected herself into her world. Tera told her mom everything. That was until she came out.

Tera made her way back down the hall, pausing, still not making out the conversation, but guessing Cathy could be on the other line. A supposition of a trip. A getaway. It was all highly possible. But Tera's mom's offhanded comment in the car yesterday was simply that, errant. She had no plans. She didn't have friends in Maine.

After Tera used the facilities and flushed, she paused at the door, where her mom had gone silent. She had hung up the phone. She could hear her shuffling in the sheets, trying to find a comfortable spot on an uneven mattress. The creaks of the bed were louder than Tera's shuffle back into her room.

In bed, Tera rolled over and put her arm around Casey's waist. "It's good to be here."

"Yes, Tera. It's great," Casey said, moaning in her sleep. "Now let me rest. We have a big day." A snore followed and then she grunted awake again.

"I get it. It's…I want to make sure," Tera said.

"It's fine. You're so obsessed. It'll be fine." Casey cradled in her spot and then the snores began again.

Tera wrestled with the sheets for the third time that week. She raised her right arm in the air and let it dangle there, elbow stiff and straight. She felt the weight and what little she had to do to balance it. It wasn't meditation, but concentration on nothing. She tried to find peace. And within this odd but calming movement, she found relaxation.

Sometimes she got angry. Yes, she had some anger management issues. But she took time, took pause, not to meditate like the counselors had said in high school. She would never take their suggestions literally. She didn't like to be told what to do. But she found quiet time, whether at 3:00 a.m. or in the middle of the day, by simply clasping her hands and tuning the world out. She wasn't sure if she could survive if she didn't. And in that pause, she felt release. She returned to it when she got angry and tried to find the moment that she could be quiet with herself and counteract the anger.

CHAPTER 11

The house was rather quiet when Pauline woke up. She muddled around the kitchen, picking at the rust around the intersection of the faucet and the sink like her daughter had done. This would be a day. She needed to prepare herself for the inevitable stress. It was pent up, unresolved childhood trauma. Trauma that had to have been Pauline's fault, although she absolutely couldn't pinpoint it. The passive aggressive comments directed at everyone except Monica were frustrating. Pauline couldn't retort. The comments were so soft, so stingingly quiet. She could only put on a motherly voice and cradle Tera with her words, hoping it helped.

When Pauline's husband left, it damaged them both. Pauline didn't have coping mechanisms for any of the various points throughout time. The divorce group provided little help. When she went to see a psychiatrist, he only wanted to see what was wrong with Pauline. Pauline simply stated that the only things wrong were with her husband. She made four visits and canned the whole attempt. Pauline tried to rely on Samantha, but she really found her to be self-involved. She couldn't care more than to listen to a few words and then change the topic to her and Robert.

Pauline struggled those first few years. She struggled with loneliness and finding friends, a daughter figuring out her sexuality, and abandonment. The abandonment was the only thing she got over. She might not rush into a relationship so quickly again. Not as she had with her husband. She checked her lists of requirements twice and made sure the people she let in were there for life and for her daily.

It's true, she talked to everyone. Started up conversations with strangers in the department stores, the grocery store bagger, and clerks after a robbery. People online. That's how she got over the loneliness. But people in for the long-haul, she reserved for a longer process of vetting. She had a list. She actually made sure the person was good to bring into her life and Tera's life as well. Now Casey and Monica's life. She checked the list regularly. She would not be left behind again.

Pauline pulled her palms up to the air and held them on the sink ledge, arm's width apart. They were still damp with sink water. She hadn't bothered to dry them. If she believed in God, she would ask that he grant her patience. She wasn't sure though if she could ask for anything given that she hadn't been to a church in over five years, missing even the major holidays.

Pauline took in a gasp, paused for three stops, and then blew the air fully out. She repeated and then repeated and found her center, found her calm. The day would be difficult, but she must get through it no matter how counterproductive it ended up being.

Casey trudged in, eyes half closed, and said with a start, "Good morning." Her eyes opened a little wider after Pauline's chirped response, an echo of Casey's. Casey immediately got to work pulling out pans and butter and a large crate of eggs. Soon, the warmth of the stove hit Pauline as she sat in the chair. She promised to do the dishes because she was so delighted to be cooked for and served.

When Monica surfaced from her room and slid into a seat at the rudimentary kitchen table, Pauline was already eating her eggs and bacon. An English muffin rounded out the plate, making it count as a full meal. "Good morning," Monica said.

"Good morning. It's so nice to see you." Pauline whispered the words, hoping to not wake Tera just yet.

"Tera is sleeping in. She'll be up soon. She's so excited to be on this vacation with you both." Casey gushed and flicked the frying pan a bit. As she reached to place the muffins in the toaster she said, "This is just so important to her."

The day got off to a good start by Pauline's measure. Everyone was keeping their sanity. When Tera inevitably rose, she was in a good mood. Pauline chastised her a bit for sleeping in and Tera could only retort that for her it was a vacation too.

The group piled into the car for the trip to the first winery. They had planned ten for this their first day on the wine trail. Everyone had pretzels on hand. Monica had saltines. A joke barf bag made its way around the car as they were leaving. It would be Pauline's day to drive.

The first winery was a small establishment with only a room in an open vineyard. The landscape was certainly the draw and not the building. A big picture window showed the breadth of the associated land, the well. It stretched for quite a distance before the lake poked out of the horizon. The hill rolled gently down to the water's level with rows of vines with grapes dotting the branches that hung on wooden framing. They chattered that they wanted to walk down to it, but they just hadn't the strength. After a few drinks. Pauline didn't have the right shoes.

Another winery proved to be a simple bar with no view. They all pouted for a bit because the view at the first winery had been so spectacular. Monica raised they might all go back and have a full pour. Maybe another day. Casey simply responded that there were so many places to see.

"Yeah, with no views," Monica said. She pouted her bottom lip.

They clad the winery in silver. Everything shimmered in the vein of a medieval theme. A coat of arms of an Italian variety adorned the walls and seared on the countertops. Everyone cheered that this was the best tasting winery despite the gimmicky Italian and silver theme. The suit of armor tackily hung on a hook next to the coat rack. This was nothing like Italian wine. The bartender, when asked, replied that the family had moved from Italy, but they too agreed that Italian wine did not compare. The wine sparked tastebuds like no other. Somehow that appeased the room.

Monica, Casey, and Pauline checked out with several bottles each. Tera refused. She said the graphics and decor were just too much. It ate at her soul, she said.

"Hard pass," Tera said as they left. She jumped off the boat.

By the fifth winery, three of them were all a little tipsy. The cheese snacks didn't go far, and they planned on lunch at a restaurant nearby. They had gathered at least twelve bottles of wine between them, and they all joked that they wouldn't have room in the trunk for their luggage soon. They wouldn't.

"What's your poison, a brassy lady?" the bartender said, and she leaned in on Monica.

"Well. I'm not as good at this, so I've been taking recommendations from whoever is pouring."

"Ma'am, you're not meant to be good at it. You just must kick it back and enjoy."

"I guess I don't want to make a fool of myself or throw up," Monica said.

"Oh, you won't. You won't," The bartender said. "And if you do, you do."

Pauline, Casey, and Tera all lined up with two others attending to the group's wants and desires.

"Well. Let's try the Riesling. Because to be honest, it's the Finger Lakes. Right. You've gathered that much."

"Yes. That's what they've all been saying."

"We also have this dry red that is really the best for the area. It's worth a taste. Are you interested?" the bartender said.

"Yes. I do like dry wine. It makes my tongue stick to the roof of my mouth." She giggled as the girls listened in.

She poured these and one other semi-sweet and showed Monica the order of events. They chatted mostly about the woman behind the bar and how she got there. Imported from Missouri, she followed her husband.

"My ex-husband wouldn't approve, but that's why I'm here. He's over in Ithaca doing something in tech. I don't need him, anyway. Would say I'm wasting my life away. I'd say I'm being refined," Pauline said.

"I'm also single and mingling," Monica said as she sipped

the first glass. "I'm so glad the girls have taken us on this trip. It's really a true getaway and is bringing me back into my own."

"You could find a man here, even. Just keep looking. You can tell who has wallets."

When she got to the third glass, she took a sip and then gulped. "It's better than sex." Monica wiped the drool on her sleeve and they both set into raucous laughter.

The girls shot glances at Monica as she tilted her head back and laughed again. "You're stealing all the attention, Mom," Casey said.

Pauline lurched over and put her arm in Monica's. "You're having too much fun, dear. Another round, ma'am," she said with a sultry stare into the bartender's eyes. "This better be good."

"We were just talking about sex with exes, ma'am," the bartender said.

"Well, of course I'm in, dear. Let's make this good," Pauline said.

After they finished carousing and boozing, the group ate lunch at a fancy restaurant next to the winery.

They spent too much money and were gluttonous. Tera had ordered the charcuterie board to start, and they were all full after they pecked at it. Pauline said she was full before they brought the food out. They had cheese snacks all day. Still, they got the charcuterie board, and the server put it in a takeout container before they left. It would make good leftovers, to put in eggs, Tera had remarked.

"I'll hear none of it. This place has the best meats and cheeses," Tera had said.

Pauline picked up the tab, but not after Tera made a fuss that it wasn't right, and she and Casey could afford to pick up the tab. It seemed to Pauline to be a ploy, so she simply took the check and removed herself to go up to the register and pay. Despite this, it seemed to put Tera in a sour mood.

Pauline could overhear Tera fighting with Casey from the distance of the register. She couldn't believe they were doing it in front of Monica. It was so childish. Pauline darted eyes back every second she could, as she handed over the check, as she gave her card, as she signed the bill. Then, when the duty was done, she stormed back to the table to scold the girls for bickering in plain view of a mother.

"Mom, we were just discussing," Tera said.

"It's not appropriate Tera. Monica doesn't want to hear you squabble."

"It's an unpleasant fact, Mom. There's nothing more to it. It's a way of life. Everyone does it."

"Look, I can see you're making Monica uncomfortable," Pauline said.

"You are making Monica uncomfortable," Tera said.

When they grew tired of squabbling amongst themselves, they all headed back to the car. Casey and Tera had their arms folded almost in a pout. But not Pauline. She was still driving, now sober as a cop. She apologized gently for losing it, and they took off to the next spot. Monica said she hoped they would find better cheese because although the wine was spectacular, the cheese was less than desirable.

Casey wanted to go to all the wineries, so she put up her argument. She stumbled back to the vehicle and held the door comically, not getting in. She clapped her hands. "One more," Casey said.

"But the cheese is no good." Casey's mom also slurred her words.

"Of course, we're going to more," Tera said. "Get in the car and we'll go."

"Trapped you." Tera giggled.

Casey fumbled for the door and then relaxed. "One more." She stamped her feet on the floor, this time seated.

They partook of another winery and then one more, and it did Casey in for the day. She fell asleep on the leather seats on the way to their next destination. Pauline felt they needed to take a break and stop drinking for an hour. She would've been fine if they all took a nap right there at that moment.

CHAPTER 12

In the late afternoon, a hike was on the agenda. They all agreed, despite being tipsy, that they could do the short hike. Pauline had mumbled something and crossed her arms. Monica glared at her with a hard stare. "Speak up," she said.

The daughters looked on pleadingly. The hard looks won. There was a mountain close by in a nearby town that was frequented by the locals. They would park at the top and walk down. They hoped to get the shuttle van at the base to take them back up to their car. It was supposed to be an hour hike down.

Although they all chimed in about how it would be such a show-stopping activity at first, when they got to the top and got out of the car, Pauline immediately dissented. "Well, I'm not dressed for this," Pauline said as Casey kicked summit rocks, looking over the cliffs. "I'll ruin my boots."

"We told you this morning that this was part of the agenda," Tera commented. "They're chunky heeled boots, but their boots no less. It should be fine."

They told Pauline several times her shoes would be fine, she wouldn't even scuff them, and Pauline held a stiff face each time. She didn't complain, but the words and planned events rumbled in the back of her brain as she processed them.

"I didn't even bring the proper shoes in the first place. This is the best I have." Pauline blushed a little in embarrassment in front of Monica. "Tera, how could you not have told me? And with how organized you are."

She wore linen slacks, and a short sleeve designer sweater. Of course, these items were prone to mud and stains. Even the dry cleaner could have trouble getting the linen slacks clean. And her thick chunky sole was one thing, but the way the shoes were loose on her feet was another. She rolled her ankles around for Tera, making a point.

"It'll be fine, Mom. It's all downhill."

"Downhill. That's right. The trip from here on out is downhill."

They scrambled across rocks and loose dirt at the top of the trail. Pauline had the most trouble. The dirt gathered in small step like ledges, but it became apparent the dirt was loose in some areas.

"This is not—"

"Oh, come on, it will be fun, Mom. Let loose. Go out of your comfort zone. Please," Tera said.

"Oh boy. This is too much for sure. I'll never make it down." After some more hoots and hollers, they were on their way past the treacherous top.

For several stretches of terrain, they were fine, but about fifteen minutes in, there was a crack that all four of them heard. Pauline, in the pack's rear, flopped down on the dirt. This was something she would never do because she dressed for a winery and though the pants were casual, they were also probably several hundred dollars. The oversized short-sleeved sweater jacket that she wore was probably another several hundred.

"This is not good Pauline."

They all looked back, stopped in their tracks.

Tera came over and, in a motherly way, tried to stretch the ankle forward and slightly to the side. It had swelled and was swelling increasingly.

"That is not pleasant," Pauline said, turning her head away.

"Just let me see." Tera gingerly touched the swelling.

Pauline winced in pain. "I think you mean to say: 'emergency vehicles don't come up here. Get up, let's go. Or we need to keep moving.'" Tears bubbled in Pauline's eyes.

"Mom. I think it's just sprained. We. We'll figure this out." At her side, Tera asked her mom to stretch her ankle and roll it in circles.

Pauline could do neither.

"Well, we will just have to go get help," Monica said.

"Yup. I think that's the only thing." Casey stared at her phone. "No cell service."

Pauline flopped her hands on the ground in disapproval.

"Ok. It's only about five miles. We'll wait here. Send someone to the top to come down and get us. I can't carry Mom back up it, but some other hunk of a man might." Tera raised her eyebrows and bit her lips. "You'd like that right, Mom?"

"Well…" Pauline said, hanging on her thoughts and her words.

When they were gone, Tera moved in to hold her mom. "It'll be okay. Mom. We'll get out of this."

Tears rolled down Pauline's face. "This is why I don't enjoy hiking." She mouthed the word 'fuck.'

"I really don't think you've ever held me," Tera said. "Mom, I know we're not that close. Never really been that close. But I want to change that. I want us to be comfortable around each other. Never on edge."

"Absolutely, dear. We were close when you were a child. When you grew into a teenager, you were off and never came back. You leaped into college, happy to get out of a broken home. I was left there by myself." More tears formed in Pauline's eyes.

"It seems you've finally grown up, but I'm not sure. I thought you were gone for sure. I thought you had abandoned me, too," Pauline said.

"Mom, I would never. My exploration of myself was long-lived—"

"Started at fifteen. Still happening," Pauline said.

"I never wanted to hurt you. I can see now I hurt you," Tera said.

"I just, dear, I miss you," Pauline said. "Let's start over. Have a new era of Pauline and Tera."

"Mom. I've lied to you. That's how I'm starting this relationship. I'm coming clean."

"Of course you have, dear. We all must lie sometimes."

"Number one: smoking. I smoked well past the time I told you I quit. When I would come home. I would sneak out to the garage. I'd go out just past the garage. Once or twice, I turned on the shower and the fan and smoked out the bathroom window. I put the butt in the toilet and flushed."

"Oh, dearie, this isn't necessary. I know. I always knew."

"Right. I felt so bad. But it was an addiction, right? It was so hard to beat. I have quiet now. Casey has helped me."

"Oh, and I'm to believe that." Pauline giggled through the pain of her ankle, grabbing it as she laughed and jostled her body.

"Casey really is good for me, even if we bicker. It's just that we want to resolve things right away, not keep things bottled up, right?"

"Absolutely, dearie. It's just appearances are everything. Remember that."

"Mom. Somehow, I felt you wouldn't understand."

A squirrel dashed from the bushes across the path, paused and lifted its front end, then jerked some looks before scuttling off. Pauline screamed as it left, late, almost as if it took longer than a few moments to register because it was so foreign.

"Mom. It's just a squirrel."

Despite the trouble they were both in, the view was gorgeous. Just like the bumper stickers said. Greens swirled with yellows, and dew and a babbling small stream complimented it all. Pauline, for a moment, forgot herself and imagined that her daughter, Tera, also forgot herself. Her constant headache, her consternation.

Pauline watched as Tera sat on her butt and twisted a small green branch into knots. As the stem cracked, a bit of dewy juice would glaze the sides. Tera didn't seem to care and only once wiped her hand on her thigh.

"Remember that boy. The one I almost killed myself for?" Tera said.

"Dear, what do you mean? Mark? That's the only boy I ever knew. The only one you ever brought home. Dear, let's not get started about this, about that boy. The one who could've been, eh? Was that the deal?" Pauline rustled through her purse, which she had almost instinctively brought with her, looking for something. Something that would tell her what way they were going. A pamphlet picked up carelessly or an agenda supplement from the girls. She needed a tidbit about how to find help or rest or transportation home. She pushed aside lipstick and pens, a notepad and wallet, rummaging.

"I came out because that's who I was, Mom. That was months after he finally left me alone. It was when he didn't that I thought about dying. When he didn't get the hint." Plain faced, Tera glanced at her and almost met her eyes.

The shuffling stopped, and Pauline charted her eyes, confirmed she was stuck where she was. Avoiding Tera's eyes and words, half-listening, she bent over the branch of a nearby tree. She bent it as much as she could, but it did not break. "We can all bend branches, peel bark." And Pauline set to whittling her own stick for distraction.

Standing silently, Tera sniffed. The noise echoed to the sun and back.

On this new day, they had nowhere to go.

"Really, I never meant to try to ease you back into men. I was so horrible. There're things I realize now. Some considered it a suicide scare, wasn't it? Because of him? You simply scared yourself? Unruly? Dearie, everyone gets hurt. Surely you get that now from Marina?"

Pauline knew about Marina, Tera's first stable girlfriend. She heard. Tera told her about her sadness. Pauline latched onto those few words Tera ever gave her, the little insight into Tera's life. She always had the wrong answer. Pauline knew she would never measure up to being a good mom. She could never replace the daughter she had before she contemplated suicide.

"I never figured out how to handle your sexuality, dear." Pauline muttered the words. "I was so conflicted myself. How was I to even guess?"

"Mom, I always dated boys. I grew up with boys. We played nonstop because the girls didn't like me. Do you know why they didn't like me? Because I was gay…tomboyish," Tera said.

"If I could go back now, dear, I would," Pauline said.

"Look. I'm over it. It's just…to be honest…you still stress me out. It seems there's nothing I can do sometimes. Right?"

"Dear. I'll try to back off this week. Do you want me to go?" Pauline asked.

"No. Mom, I could never. It's just we all need to chill," Tera said. "It's not a big deal if Casey and I squabble."

Tera picked up a few rocks and aimed them at a spot of red spray paint on a rock about one-hundred yards away. She flung each one like a skimming rock at the dot. As she spoke to her mom, the rocks ticked away. Her eyes were damp.

"Just because I cried, cry, because I was sad. You all automatically assumed I wanted to die. Disappear, yes. Go somewhere." Clink. Pauline's eyes moved to the rock where out of the corner of her eye she saw Tera hit the target. Then she stopped flinging.

Tera looked up and back at her mom. "Fine, someone yes. But the place I was stuck in was dampening. Of course, I started a suicide scare. But it never, ever, became my intent not to live. Not to be somewhere with some specific person. I mean, it's one thing to have a rock chucking talent. Why would you not want to live?"

"Oh dear. That boy and you were no good together. You were such hoodlums. You were always in trouble. How was I supposed to react to get you to be better, be good? If I was 'dampening,' it was only because I loved you."

Tera moved back to chuck her rocks. There was no peace between them until Tera heard Casey's voice and jumped up with a revived positive energy.

When Casey and Monica made it back with two rather large Forest Rangers, Pauline was less than enamored. "Be careful. I'm not a piece of meat, boys." The men gripped Pauline by the shoulders to lift her.

She naturally put her arms around their shoulders, raised her left foot, bent at the knee. The two men helped her step by step, or hop by hop, up the hill. Pauline felt she had no weight. Most of it was distributed on the hunky shoulders of the men: 5'11, 185 pounds, biceps she never yet imagined existed. Still, she wasn't interested at all. What would she do with a Forest Ranger? Didn't they like to climb mountains and do earthy things? No, thank you.

With an odd hop, her other ankle turned, and the world was over. She cursed aloud the spirits of the forest and pulled her right arm off a shoulder to wipe the tears now streaming from her face.

"It's fine. Can you add weight? If you can't, we'll carry you," the bigger ranger said.

And they could have. They were strong enough. And Pauline would have preferred it because it was less work and because her emotions were debilitating her more than the ankle. All six of them knew Pauline would trudge on. She would never ask them to carry her. She would at least try. Tears all the way.

When they got to the top, Tera made a joke: "Is this how you pick up men, Mom? No, they really picked up you." No one laughed quite like Tera, entirely amused by herself. The lack of laughter pulled her back to reality, and she asked if her mom wanted to take the rest of the day off, ice up. That's what she had done when she twisted her ankle on ice last winter.

The men edged her toward the car, sat her down in the back seat, and slung her legs over into the open area. What had taken them fifteen minutes to descend took more like forty-five minutes to ascend to the starting point.

"Thank you both," Pauline said, dusting off her lap. She reached into her purse for some cash that would've gone to bartenders.

"Oh, we can't, ma'am," The one hunk said.

"We're just happy you're safe," the shorter said in an upright tone.

Tera came to her side and patted her shoulder. "You'll be all right, Mom. I'm sure of that. Let's go back to the house of trash and ice up."

Pauline, through the pain, could sense the love of her daughter. The moment they shared on the mountain. A place Pauline had never gone but maybe wanted to go to in another life. Her daughter was a woman now, who was not always so great with words. She felt the warmth, but the words bit and stuck in her head.

CHAPTER 13

When they got back to the place where they were staying, Pauline grabbed an empty sandwich bag out of a sparsely stocked drawer to apply ice to her ankle. She could finally settle down and relax. She was in heaven, just resting. The woods incident caused trauma. Not only did mud and bugs bother her, but even the scent of sap and green growth. It repulsed her. She would take a bath if it were any other place, relax in the faux scents of lavender or sage, or even pine. It would be so much better removed from dirt and bugs.

She nestled into a small cove in her bedroom. There was a cushiony chair, which was an odd addition considering the sparse furniture. It was as if it were waiting there for her to come home with her bum ankle. In some regards, because of that one accoutrement, a comfortable side chair and ottoman, everything was just perfect. Once positioned, she bent at the waist and adjusted the bag of ice on her ankle.

Tera entered through the open door. Pauline thought about the effort it would take to close it just for a bit. She needed a bit of a timeout. A second to gather herself and her thoughts, but here was Tera, her golden child with a bright face.

"You'll be fine, Mom. I'm sure it will be almost better by tomorrow," Tera said.

Pauline could rotate the ankle now and although there were a few spots of purple, she hoped she could walk on it. She had come through the door almost just fine.

"Are you sure you didn't fake an injury to get the attention of hunky park rangers?"

"Absolutely sure," Pauline said in a sing-song way.

She relaxed in her bedroom, leg outstretched with a bag of ice as she balanced on the ankle, turning her leg when it got a little too cold.

"Dear, did you mean those things in the woods?" Pauline asked. "Was it my fault?"

"No, Mom. It wasn't totally your fault. No one recognized I was gay. It was society's fault. You are a part of society. But do you get what I'm saying?"

"Yes. I think so, dear." Pauline entirely didn't. She picked at her cuticles and looked up.

"I did love you. I do love you. It, I just, was a long time ago. I just wanted you to be like the other girls." Pauline wiped at her eyes. "I really didn't know."

"Mom. It was the cigarettes that started it. You probably associated the alternative lifestyles with dreadful things like cigarettes. That was probably it," Tera said.

"Yes. Dear, it probably was." Pauline shook her head from side to side.

Tera walked swiftly past her mother on her way to leave the room, probably to go to her bedroom. "This conversation isn't over, Tera," Pauline said as Tera disappeared. Pauline could not follow.

"Reading a book," Tera said from her bedroom. "On the one piece of furniture in my room."

Pauline relaxed and felt her pain as she lifted her leg and ankle to readjust. Someone would have to get her a fresh bag of ice soon. The water dripped from the corners, wetting her ankle and the ottoman. What was a little water on a cheap ottoman in a dump of a house? Hadn't they all agreed that it was, in fact, a piece of garbage house? Pauline would never say it aloud.

Monica popped her head into the room to check on Pauline. She wrapped her hands around the door jamb and looked in with a smile. It was cutesy, but it got Pauline. "Come on in, Monica."

"How are you doing? I was so worried on the way down," Monica said.

"You could've stayed with Tera and I," Pauline said. "It might've steered the conversation to less dramatic topics."

"What do you mean?" Monica asked.

"Oh, nothing. It's just we had some mother-daughter moments that were kind of intense."

"I understand that," Monica said candidly. "Before my husband and I split, Casey and I would get into fights that knocked each other with words. It was worse than the blows my husband gave me."

"Oh, I'm sorry. I didn't realize," Pauline said.

"Oh, it's not. I didn't mean to over share. It's just…Casey really saved me. If she didn't convince me to leave, I probably never would have," Monica said, now slimming her slacks with her hands. "I was stuck. They trap you in there." She leaned in, and said almost in a whisper, "There's no other way to get out. They'll threaten you and convince you to stay. Apologize after they hit you. They'll bring flowers. I got flowers every time, and it was flattering. I almost enjoyed getting them because I had known they would be coming."

"Oh, Monica. I had it bad, but I'm so sorry," Pauline said.

"No, it's okay. My daughter was the reason I got out. I'll never let it happen again. I saw the signs."

Monica turned to walk away, but she lingered in the doorway. "I just. I want to make sure you're okay, Pauline. Daughters can be a handful. They have the power to turn tears on. Just be careful. We'll all get through it." Monica escaped down the hallway.

Pauline felt what Monica meant. Tera could have a mouth, and she was aware of how to pull strings. She was still her daughter, a bit too much like her mother. Pauline knew now, though, that Monica noticed the behavior. That it was disruptive. She blushed in embarrassment. Her daughter and her still had some things to work out.

Minutes later, her bag of ice had become a wet and dripping problem. "Tera." Pauline sung out down the hallway. "I need a fresh bag. Can you help me?"

Tera clumped to her feet as she came across the hall back into the room. She entered, almost stomping her feet like she had when she was twelve and Pauline wouldn't buy her new shoes, seeing that the ones she had were only six months old.

Her feet had the same sound, ring, or perhaps the same feeling resulted. Pauline felt the vibration of a foot on the floor. As a kid, Tera stomped on the back of her sneakers until they caved. Ragged and torn, they became an eyesore. It forced Pauline to give to her will. They went shopping and bought a rather expensive pair. Six months later, the pattern repeated, except this time they patronized Super Shoes. Tera had never been so appalled. Pauline bought a nice pair of Chuck All Stars, and all was well. The incident never happened again.

"Dear. I need a fresh bag of ice," Pauline said.

"I would be happy to do it, your majesty," Tera said with a bow.

"I'm incapacitated right now, dear. Please bear with me."

"Absolutely. Nothing I'd rather do right now," Tera said.

Her attitude was insufferable in Pauline's opinion. Perhaps it was being with your mom or the extra added pressure of performing for a girlfriend and her mom. Either way, it was visibly getting to Tera. She couldn't handle this kind of trip.

Tera reentered with a fresh bag of ice. This one was double bagged. She had tied a big grocery bag around a new Ziplock. "I probably just should have brought the frozen Brussels sprouts. You know?"

Tera paused and smiled at her mom. She shrugged, almost as if it didn't matter. "Mom, I hope you get better. We have a lot of trekking around to do," Tera said.

"It's already almost better, dear," Pauline said. She rolled her ankle in a big arch. "I just want to make doubly sure so I can keep up with you and Casey and Monica. That's why I'm icing it."

Later that evening, the police from the authority of the armed robbery they witnessed, called. Pauline answered and was happy to chat with them. They asked some standard questions, mostly they were just confirmations, and they let her go. They thanked her for her time and said they might ask her to come in to view mug shots at some point. The culprit might be a repeat offender. Pauline said she'd be happy to, but she reminded him he wore a ski mask, and she lived rather far away. She was on vacation now. It wasn't pressing and the officer simply said if they needed her, he might call her again and request a special trip.

"The police called," Pauline said, surfacing from the bedroom.

Tera and Casey paused and looked at Pauline in question at first but soon relaxed.

"They just wanted some details, someone to confirm the clerk didn't take the money or have knowledge of who the robber was. I think he just wanted to check and see if it looked like an inside job. He said we shouldn't have left the scene of the crime but said they would let it go."

"It's not our fault they got robbed," Tera said. "Maybe if someone got shot. Otherwise, I'm going to be on my way. Probably, happens all the time. Bank robberies, even, happen more frequently than you'd expect."

Pauline nodded in concurrence with her daughter's offhanded statements. Then she lifted her ankle and pointed down at it. "Look, all better." Pauline circled her ankle, showing progress.

"You should still keep icing it, Mom," Tera said.

"Would be a good idea." Casey chimed in.

"Who's the adult and who's the child?" Pauline said.

Tera was setting the table for the steak dinner Casey had prepared. She just came in from the grill with a plate of four perfectly browned steaks. The lines were impeccable. They could be caricatures of themselves. The accompanying corn and potatoes looked delicious, and they soon devoured the lot.

When they were done, Tera cleared the table, and Monica did the dishes. "Relax, relax," they said to Pauline.

"Here. Take this fresh bag of ice," Tera said.

Pauline retired to her room, left out and unhelpful. She would help in the morning, she told herself, even though she knew she wouldn't. She hopped more than stood on her one leg and put her weight on various objects: a chair, the doorknob, a wall. When she finally got back to her resting spot, which nobody had actually helped her get to, she heard Tera and Monica both call out separately,

"Are you all right?" Tera said.

When Pauline did not respond, Monica yelled, "You get back to your spot, okay?"

"Yes. Oh, yes. Fine. Thanks." Pauline sunk into the cushion and sighed. Somehow, she had obtained some additional alone time. She paged through her book, but she didn't want to commit to it. She yawned and leaned back, wondering if the ice would fall or melt if she slept. It had been a long day. The events had piled up and now she wanted to decompress, pretend it didn't happen, sleep.

CHAPTER 14

Casey usually woke up early and would not instinctively start any one activity. She muddled about. She often made Tera a fabulous breakfast or bought something special from a nearby bakery or restaurant. The gesture always felt glorious, and Tera relished the acts of service.

That day, Tera woke up early, likely because she had so much trouble sleeping. She thought about her mom and what she could be hiding. The vacation festered. Everyone felt the stale emptiness of the house. A group of smokers might've been the last guests. She looked at Casey and slowly let out the air. She had let on to Casey just how bad it really was.

"See, it's not so bad," Casey said. "There's a bakery. The whole vacation, we're going to have sweet breakfasts. Couldn't ask for a better location if you ask me."

"I guess. Well, it's not perfect, but at least we have danishes," Tera said. She looked frantically for the notebook she had rifled through last night but could not find it. Her mom had moved it to a more discrete location.

"How's your foot?" Casey said.

"Oh. It's much better. I really could've gotten down that hill. I didn't get a merit badge yesterday, but someday maybe we can try again."

"It's good to hear," Casey said. "I'm just so sorry yesterday turned out like it did…danish?"

"I'm just happy with a cup of joe." Tera's mom took a big swig out of the ceramic mug, one that the hosts might've stolen from a three-star hotel breakfast bar: the uniformly tan but speckled kind with a chunky handle and thick cup.

The coffee was Maxwell House and Tera knew what that meant without drinking it. Thin and bland, brown hot water. Tera would have a headache. All four of them liked a robust Columbian or dark roast. The stuff that costs ten dollars a bag. It was an interlude of conversation in the car just the day before.

"Mom…" The word trailed off like a child complaining. Tera's mom was being performative. She had never drunken coffee, guzzled it out of anything besides an expensive paper cup from a café. A skinny latte with vanilla was her drug of choice. Somehow, she got the swill down.

Casey's mom chimed in. "Let's get this going girls."

In a few brief minutes, they all piled into the car. Casey's mom took her spot in the back right, just as usual. Tera started the car, replacing her slightly incapacitated mom, and they were off. Casey would take over driving if Tera got too drunk. They had all agreed on this.

"I'm fine, really. It's just a little tender," Pauline said.

"You're faking it."

"What? Faking the injury or the recovery."

"Both," Tera said.

Tera could only imagine driving the sixty-thousand-dollar convertible into a giant lake while she was drunk, so she kept the task at bay and hoped they all wouldn't down too many samples, that she would eat enough cheese.

They stopped at a roadside stand and got some fresh produce to go with the sweet breakfasts for the week: apples, blackberries, and pears. The woman behind the cart simply smiled and took the cash. She didn't appear to have anything to say, and the group didn't have questions. It was a frequent transaction, Pauline was sure. As they left, the woman swayed and sent a quick wave at the car.

"So quaint."

Tera was in a mood, and retorted, "That job is probably important to her, Mom. You shouldn't call her quaint. She depends on that money, I'm sure." She turned the steering wheel and sped off. A trail of dust appeared behind her.

Pauline picked at one carton of berries. They had taken all but one berry and left a few apples. The woman's day would be about over.

They stopped at a winery, indulging in a cheese bisque

soup and cheesecake and raspberry tart. Barrels surrounded the room on three sides, and the center held a single bartender behind a barricade of more barrels. A small opening allowed the bartender to escape as needed.

"This is so pleasant," Pauline said. "We have the place to ourselves. I'm so glad we're with you girls. This could be no better than it is." She gushed.

"What can I serve you?" the bartender asked.

She was the owner and came out and served for unique events. After living in California for most of her life, she returned to the east coast where she grew up. That was ten years ago. She and her husband bought a winery to bring something more than Rieslings to the area.

"Oh, I love dry reds. I'm so glad…" Pauline leaned in and winked at the bartender. "We'll get along just fine."

"Just happens to be our specialty," the bartender said.

"Are you flirting—Mom?" Tera lengthened the sentence with a trailing M.

They all tested the dry reds, and Monica smacked her tongue against the roof of her mouth in disapproval. "I prefer sweet," she said.

"We have mostly dry wine, but you ought to try Fruit Made. It's a meadery and I'm sure it will suit your tastes."

Four wineries in and Tera mentioned the house again. Her dissatisfaction. They all sat in the car and had a moment with Tera. She wouldn't call the rental host. She wouldn't ask for a refund. They all piped up about the things they needed to go on, or not go on, during the rest of the trip stay. They would all make do. And it was decided. They all unbuckled in unison, ready to enter the Great Escape Winery.

As they entered the Jimmy style themed winery, they giggled.. There was a purple parrot and kitschy mugs. A complete wall of snarky, inappropriate t-shirts. Of course, Tera was anything but dismayed.

She whispered to her mom, "This place is so unclassy."

"It's not that bad," Tera's mom said.

"It's nothing to worry about. Got to love a purple parrot,"

Casey's mom said.

Tera turned and folded her arms. "Let's skip this one." She smiled a lean, self-satisfactory smile and then bit her lips. She was not moving.

"Tera." Casey eyed her up and down and asked her quietly to go over out of the way to talk. "My mom loves Jimmy. How could you even? You're so stuck up. So, Miss Prissy. I'm finally seeing who you are."

The only words Tera heard were stuck up, prissy. "Who do you think you are? This place isn't worth my while. Did you see how embarrassed my mom is? It's so embarrassing."

"I can't believe you." Casey was furious.

"Come on. Let's go," Pauline said.

"What? Go where? They're fighting. I don't even care about this place. I don't even really like Jimmy."

"Let's teach them a lesson. Come on, let's go."

Casey's mom threw her hands up in the air and made for the door, following close behind Tera's mom.

At the car, they struggled with the convertible top for a moment. It looked like it might even rain and spoil the day another way. They giggled as they worked on the top.

"Just pull this lever and the top will go down," Pauline said.

"They're going to notice we left."

"I know. I just really want to do this."

And the top was down, and Monica and Pauline scrambled into the car. Pauline let out the loudest yell possible. "Screw you girls! We're having fun."

***

Monica's arms rose and the tips of her fingers must've felt the push of the now cool, flowing air. They had broken free.

Besides a few more hoots and hollers and a slowdown to check out two local anglers alongside the banks of the lake, they were quiet.

"His butt though," Monica said.

Pauline glanced with her eyes peeking out from the tops of her sunglasses and sucked her lips in. A hard breath emerged and then she sped up, leaving the scene.

When they got back to the house, they entered through the chic, bold front door, absent a wreath or any ornament at all. They simultaneously flopped into the chairs in a makeshift living room. Each was a distinct thrift store purchase from a different era. Monica got a mid-century woven cushion oversized chair. Pauline picked an early fast casual restaurant metal bistro chair. They were both uncomfortable.

"What, we just leave them there?" Monica said.

"They'll duke it out, maybe take the day to themselves. They'll find their way home. Ubers, right? We never had Ubers when we were that age. Well, if you got out of a hungry man's car at the top of a dark secluded hill, you were walking home." She ran her fingers along the cool metal chair. It was sturdy, after all. "They'll work it out. They better because they are the ones really ruining the trip."

Monica finished the dishes. A few more had gathered since breakfast, including one Pauline took big gulps of water from when they returned to the house. The drying rack was under a plastic mat. When she lifted the mat, she saw water stains had seeped into the linoleum counter seams, and the edges slightly detached from a metal band capping it. The edges were peeling up, damp, and warped. Had they done that? Surely not, not if the dish rack was there the whole time. It wasn't as though they had pulled it from the cabinet underneath and put it there. Pauline watched Monica slowly lower the plastic and leave it be.

Pauline twirled her ankle again, tensing in the stretch of her joints. It cracked, and she grinned broadly. I think that was it. It's all in place now. Everything will be fine from here on out. Pauline relished her decision, the tantrum she had executed not to be outdone by her daughter ever. Tera was probably reeling in anger. She was cursing her mom. She knew it. Pauline folded her hands, pointed the palms out, and stretched. She found content and would linger there all day if she could, but she had other plans that she needed Monica to sign on to.

CHAPTER 15

Minutes after they stormed off away from their moms at the winery, Tera dropped her glass on the ledge of the windowsill. It infuriated Tera. Her face was visibly red in the sunlight and the large glass windows sent a glare right into her eyes. The furrow in her brow was not from sadness but from hate. She hated this vacation. She hated Casey because it was convenient. Her anger raged, and it was all she could do but to ball up her fist in distress. They might've turned purple if she had had the nerve to look at them.

As Tera balled her fists, Casey bitterly egged on the argument a bit more, pointing out how Tera could sing all the words to that one Jimmy song.

"Nibblin' dah, dah, sponge cake…" Casey sang.

"I can sing all the lyrics. But come on, I like sponge cake, but it's all a mockery. I'm making fun of Jimmy."

"You've got to be kidding me. You've obviously listened to the song so many times, why not turn it off when you hear it? Did you…did you at one point look up the lyrics on the internet?" Casey scoffed. She leaned in with her glaring eyes and pecked Tera on the lips.

"Shit. What are you—" Humbled, Tera melted in the moment of heat. Lunging in, she took Casey, wrapping her arms around Casey's neck and pressing hard lips to hers.

Their sex had become passionate after fights. At first, it was almost as if they got in fights to have sex. Their hormones raged with their anger and that's just the way it was. It became as much a misunderstanding.

But now, here they were in a winery. A very tacky winery. And there was nowhere to have sex. They attacked each other with unbridled hate, and there was no way to recoil this time. They couldn't let their passion go, redirect.

"Tera. We need to stop this. It's getting to be too much.

We are hurting each other with our words. Yes, the sex is great, but let's concentrate on us, making us work. Fights are not an end to a means. Especially now that I'm frustrated with nowhere to go. No bed in sight. And I'm sure you don't want to do it in a bathroom with a big ceramic parrot looking over your shoulder." Casey kicked the toes of her shoes against Tera's.

"Casey. Let's try. We're both stressed. Okay. I'm the most stressed, but you're also stressed. This is too much. It was a bad idea—"

Tera looked around the room to make eye contact with the moms, but they were gone. Casey and Tera moved toward the broad picture window looking out on the vineyards and did not see them. It was rare that people hiked through the grapes anyway, not even just for a stroll. Possibly, the owner took them on a private tour. That would be the day. Maybe if they were buyers. Tera moved to the bathroom and couldn't find either of them.

When she returned, Casey moved toward Tera with open palms at her side. "I was just at the window. Tera, the car's gone."

"What?" Tera asked her to repeat herself.

"The car is gone. The moms have left," Casey said.

"Great. Was it—It was our arguing. Fuck. The moms hate us," Tera said.

"The moms have run away," Casey said.

They both relaxed into a laugh at the whole situation.

Tera stopped over at the bar and asked for a sweet white and a semi-sweet red. It was all they had. She returned to a table where Casey situated herself, waiting. Tera bowed her head and cooed. "We will drink for the moms."

Casey chirped back. "It's our fault."

"I know," Tera said, ignoring reality. "Lift a glass to the moms and to stop our fighting. We shall never fight again. At least not without a bed around."

"Well, could be worse. We could be with a whole bridal party," Casey said. "Limo drivers have got to get so sick of those shenanigans."

Casey and Tera stayed at the winery and drank for two hours. They swayed back and forth to Jimmy songs after Tera had loosened up a bit. They made friends with some fifty-year-old might-be fans, only to find out they hated it too.

"We're just here for the booze," the man said.

"It's really not our style either way, high or low, I mean. I mean, we make good money, but we're not snotty," the wife said when Tera railed about how tacky it was to her husband.

They agreed that the wine was the most drinkable there. They had frozen fruity rum options, which weren't even conceivable at some of the other wineries. Tera sipped away, either mocking or enjoying the music the whole time. Casey pointed, opened her mouth, and then laughed deliberately, every time Tera swayed too sincerely or mouthed the words.

The woman's husband started downing shots. Tera and Casey weren't sure where they had come from, but they started throwing them back because they were almost drunk. When Tera realized she had trouble standing and couldn't find her way to the bathroom she had just looked for her mom in that, she and Casey left.

They thanked the couple for drinking rum with them and being frank about winery snobbery. He said he would stay longer because he had friends in low places.

Tera looked at him and wrinkled her nose. "You like—"

"Ahh. Got you. Isn't it an awful song?"

The girls were properly toasted when they took an Uber to the specialty grocery store to binge buy as an apology to the moms.

They meandered across the parking lot, trying their best to stay in the walking paths. People looked, stared, and children giggled as they pushed into each other and shared cheesy jokes and laughs. They weren't ready when they entered the grocery store for the bright fluorescent lights that shone down on them, and they covered their eyes once inside the automatic doors.

The aisles were ridden with junk food and somehow, they

passed it all by. They were on a mission for a four-course dinner to apologize. They make it whether or not they were drunk. The moms would forgive them if the steak burned or if it didn't.

They bought the most expensive steaks from the butcher, and a dry Italian wine and a few California semi-sweets for Monica and Casey from the liquor aisle. How truly ironic it was that they sold Italian wine at all. At one hundred dollars a bottle, it was far more expensive than any wine sold in the lakes.

The steak cuts were the good kind this time. They bought a board of deli meats and cheeses that were over a hundred dollars. All of this was an apology from the two girls. They would make it up to their moms. Tera thought she was at fault. Casey voiced her remorse and guilt. Together they had concocted the worst plan: taking their moms on a vacation. They were terribly sorry, so they bought everything they could to satiate, be gluttonous, and then they'd ask their mom's if they would like to do it again tomorrow.

Tera stood outside the grocery store with two bags of groceries. Casey held four. With one at her feet holding chilled meats, she called another Uber. Fifty minutes, it said. Fifty minutes for a ride that would take three minutes to get into a city. "Isn't this prime country for an Uber?"

"The last one took twenty minutes. We just weren't done drinking, so not that bad," Casey said.

"I can't believe this. The steaks will go bad." She called it with a tap on her phone.

They sat on a bench off to the side of the grocery store. An employee was smoking, and Tera could only think about how good the smell was. How she wished she could ask for a smoke. But that was her former self. The person who was not a runner, not a hoodlum got into trouble. She was no longer that person.

"Did you ever smoke, Casey?" Tera asked.

"Nope, never. You?" Casey responded.

"Would you still love me if I said either way?" Tera asked.

"Well, you don't know. Thank God for that. I'm not sure that we'd last if you did." Casey carried on.

"I was a hellion," Tera said. "I plagued my mom more than I ever could say. If I have kids, that shit is going to come back to me twenty-fold."

"This is what I need," Casey said. "I need you to tell me about you. Tell me things I'll never see. Who you were. Why do you have so many barriers and boundaries? I hate prying you open."

"Oh yeah, right," Tera said, responding. Something clicked. "Well, just stuff I keep bottled up. It's not savory."

"Smoked meats?" Casey said, pulling the plastic wrap off the meat and cheese platter. She eased the conversation.

"Why, I don't mind if I do."

Tera returned into the grocery store and bought a corkscrew. They opened a bottle of the Italian wine while they waited. They had botched the plan to apologize, Tera said, screw it to the whole thing. Their moms wouldn't get steak. And now…the wine was dwindling thirty minutes later, when the Uber showed up. He popped the trunk to put in half eaten groceries. The Uber driver didn't ask questions.

When they got back to the house, the moms were gone. Sitting dumbfounded for about an hour, they hoped they would return from the wineries. They could have gone to a few more. They enjoyed the company. It was possible they had stopped for dinner.

Casey reopened the loosely wrapped cheese and meat platter. "Fire up the grill."

CHAPTER 16

The pair, Monica and Pauline, partners deep in the muck, had been through quite a bit already. They had witnessed an armed robbery. They had been through the agenda fifteen times. In steady stride, they had planned breaks and quiet pauses. But most of all, they had been through several days of a weeklong bonding effort. What they could call a failed bonding effort. They all had had the best intentions but wanted something none of them could really have. Monica and Pauline watched each other fall apart with their respective daughters. Whether or not Tera was the epicenter, they were all a bit more irritable. No one felt safe in the group to be themselves. They all walked on pins.

"Can I tell you something?" Pauline took hard sips from a light tan mug. She could see the little speckles in the color of the ceramic now. They blended if you stepped away and looked at it, but she examined the matte gloss and flavor of color now, with the mug held between two hands and up to her face.

"Well, sure. I feel like we're family," Monica said. "Well, we're not really family, but we could be, might be, some day," Monica said.

"Might be. If those girls don't take each other's heads off." She adjusted the cup like a bowl onto the enamel kitchen table in front of her. Two hands carefully lowered it to its spot. "They do care about each other. I'm sure because Tera tells me. She really tries too hard, but it can be infuriating. She's obsessing, and it's maddening. That's for sure. Casey will get that."

"What is it? I'm open ears. The girls aren't home yet." She crossed her arms at her waist and leaned in, staring into her eyes from across the table. "You said you'd spill your guts, didn't you? Well, you didn't even throw up or wine," Monica said.

"Right. The girls won't be back. For all we can say, they're still Ubering around the wineries." She dipped her head hard and spoke with calm but persistent words, words meant to convince. The words had no chance right out of the gate. "Do you want to go to Maine?"

"What?" Monica inhaled and strained her eyes, squinting a bit.

Pauline looked back at them with deep intent.

"Yeah. Eventually. We could plan a trip," Monica said.

Pauline sensed Monica would rather stay.

"I mean sooner. It's a possibility, at least. This week. The rest of this weeks' vacation. The girls should get along fine without us," Pauline said.

Monica coughed. She no longer attempted to make eye contact, and her eyes moved to the floor, the kitchen window looking out into the driveway. Still, her breath was even and controlled.

"I. I met someone. Her name is Cathy, and my god is she wonderful. We met online, and she's the one person I think about nonstop. It's just that she's in trouble. Her ex is acting up again. He's poised to do something horrible. I just know it. It's an abusive thing. She really needs to leave the relationship, but I can't get her to," Pauline said. "She's not a driver and won't come see me. I have to go to her, to convince her to leave him and meet her at the same time. Introduce myself as someone who might, could, love her."

"Well. I…" Monica said. Monica took a bold and full sip and then her eyes narrowed. "I could tell you a story or two, Pauline. I know about abuse too, and you're plucking my heart strings. My husband was brutal, direct, beeline for the jaw. So that's how we ended."

"Oh, Monica. You've been through so much. Look at us, a couple of divorcees who deserved so much better, but at least we got out. Cathy didn't yet."

"He left bruises I talked about as bike accidents or the staircase. When I was a young mother, I said the kid punched me…I might have lupus, bruise easily. I'm so glad that's behind me."

"Your actual pain was physical; my abuse was psychological. I hate to say it, but this man who thinks they're still together, who Cathy just explained our relationship to, what we mean to each other, isn't yet free. And your knowledge, Monica, is so, so valuable right now," Pauline said.

"I don't know if I can do it. First, I don't want to stick myself in a situation where I'm endangered, where my physical or mental health could be endangered. And I certainly don't know if this woman, Cathy, will want my help either."

"Monica, Cathy needs all the help she can get. You would, along with me, we could…save her life. She is in actual danger."

"I do know something or two about danger. I know what it's like to not be able to brush my teeth because of all the blood and how to get a locksmith to change the locks at 2 a.m., and I also know, the most important lesson, when to call it quits with someone who is abusive—right away. That I will never unlearn. I do feel for this woman already. If I can just give her my one bit of wisdom, it might be worth it." Monica bit down and stopped talking.

"Monica, I'm so sorry." Pauline smiled hard and with energy. "We need you."

Monica was close to tears. "It might make me a better person, pull me full circle. My group, one for abused divorcees, in fact, said this might happen. I might save someone's life. I guess I could. This could be a chance to do good from all the bad that has come my way."

"It sounds ludicrous, but I've got to go. And I'd love some company. We could learn a bit more about each other. That's what the girls want, right? Haven't you ever been on an adventure, and adventure for a cause, no less?"

"It's a cause that's close to my heart. It truly is. I want to help, but we must…I'm not saying yes, but we must tell the girls," Monica said.

"Yes. I knew you would—" She cut herself off, and holding her hand in her fist, shook her hands over each shoulder in victory. "There's no place like Maine. Say it with me."

"Well, if she is in trouble. I mean, we must get her, right? It's the only thing to do." Monica closed her eyes slowly and deeply. "I'm thinking," Monica said.

"We'll just go. When the girls realize we're gone, we'll already be in Massachusetts. We will tell them it was an emergency. We just had to, for so many reasons."

Monica rose and started toward her room. "I'm just going to pack my bags. I'm not talking about this. We're just doing it. I'll be damned…The girls can learn a lesson or two about fighting in public, embarrassing the moms."

Pauline dragged her bag, already packed, out of the bedroom and into the vestibule.

To be honest, Pauline was mad at Tera. Not the same kind of anger Tera carried or the same way that she displayed it, but anger. And she wasn't immune to letting it affect her. She could act out too. She could mirror her daughter. Tera had acted like a child these first few days of the trip and it was all Pauline could do to act like a child now, for something she wanted. Tera hadn't thought about her. She took Pauline on a hike, a mountain hike. There was nothing she ever wanted to do less. She bumbled every new experience with her daughter. They ice skated once and Pauline fell every time she stood up. Tera skirted along, happy to be a kid. Lost her mom in five minutes.

And like the very first time Tera came out to her, Pauline bumbled over so many words, never quite got it out. "I love you." In the woods that day, Tera had said horrible things about her depression, about her actions while she was depressed. Yes, it hurt, and Pauline would forever remember them. It was her fault. She understood this before Tera hinted at it. She was a mother, but she felt guilt more than she could give it on this account. Tera wanted to run away from life. Ha, here was Pauline, running away from life.

When Pauline opened the door, three Dobermans came at her barking with gnarly teeth. She stepped back and slammed the door.

Monica entered the room and asked, "Is this an omen?

Should we not even go? Is the world telling us this is a bad idea?"

"Monica, you believe in Jesus. Be quiet. And a few rabid dogs have never kept me from anything." Pauline moved to the side window, opened it and yelled, "Hey." She got more attention than a car crash with her head out that cheap replacement window. The neighbors' heads turned and immediately knew who they were working with or what Pauline's goal meant to her, at the very least.

A fire rose in Pauline's blood, and she knew she appeared ever more desperate and ever more dosed with madness, calling her to get where she needed to be. "Get your fucking dogs out!" She slammed the window and pulled her head back inside. "People just never know their place. They never know how to be...rabid dogs, my Christ."

Pauline cared about Monica, and she wanted to think that Monica genuinely wanted to go. She was up for an adventure after all, wasn't she? Pauline couldn't help sometimes getting herself into an adventure.

After Monica returned to her room, gathered her toiletries from the bathroom and moved toward the door, they exited looking both ways, children crossing the street. "You'll get that woman to safety, and we'll come home. That's what we'll tell the girls, 'It's a matter of life and death.'"

"It is." Pauline scrunched her nose. "It'll be a little roomier now, for sure. We'll have space to stretch out. Oh, that Tera...the front is so much roomier. She should have offered."

"Oh, it's okay. I didn't mind. Mother and daughter, right?" Monica asked.

When they left a second time, the dogs were gone. The neighbors apparently heard them and moved them into their pens, unalarming and without comment. They must've come on their property, the rental owner's property, to do it. The women meandered out to the car and threw the bags in the back, looking the whole time for rabid dogs. They didn't see a thing.

The car felt blank to Pauline. It was a clean break from the girls, a new day with Monica. Pauline might've jerked Monica into something she didn't need to or want to be a part of, but it was all in genuine fun. Who hadn't gone on a road trip? Who hadn't skipped out on a party? That's all they were doing was having some good old-fashioned fun. "Ghosting," was what she had heard Tera call it. They were just ghosting the family vacation. No big deal.

"Maybe a little quieter, too. Without those girls always bickering." Monica spoke up for the first time about the relationship that was bugging everybody a bit more and more.

"Hindsight's 20/20 darling." She jerked the stick into reverse and pumped the pedal, stuttering backward and then pulling out onto the street. "Wahoo! Freedom."

Monica, less enthused, took off her hat and held it to her chest in reverence. She breathed in a deep breath and let the air out as Pauline watched.

"Let's hope that we don't run into any more armed robberies. I think if we avoid guns, this will be a brilliant girl's getaway. Nothing bad can happen from here on out," Monica said.

"Fuck you dogs," Monica said as they ran after the car. She flipped off the owners, who muddled about with leashes.

It was an uncharacteristic sentiment from Monica.

"Thank you, Monica. Thank you."

CHAPTER 17

The drive was pleasant. They talked only a little at first and it was the most relaxed Pauline had felt the whole week. She reveled in how great it was to have someone by her side and, at the same time, be still and silent: alone but not alone. Taking in the sights and sounds together, but not overloading the brain with contrived, forced conversation. Things that weren't meaningful.

They sat in silence for a good hour until Monica breathed in the windy air loudly at one point, starting the conversation.

"Pauline, what are your hopes and dreams?" Monica asked on the way.

"Oh, well, I guess to find my partner in crime. I guess. I'm retired and, in a way, always sunk in a bitter divorce. Of course, I want to find someone, a person who I care about, to spend the rest of my days with," Pauline responded.

They chatted about their college years and their first loves. Both let their love go. Monica had soon after college. Pauline's didn't make it through junior year.

They talked about the girls and whether it would last, whether they were each other's first loves. It was all speculation. Those were things you just could not ask. They shouldn't, but they absolutely discussed it.

"Monica, you said your husband abused you," Pauline said. "I've been thinking a lot about abuse and its many forms lately. About men. About men and abuse."

"Oh, he was the knockdown, drag it out type, Pauline," Monica said. "You know, what people say is the worst kind. Those same people talk behind your back. They have so much gumption to gossip but never want to step in. They don't want to get involved. The potential harm would be too much." Monica coughed in her fist.

"Oh, it could be they don't know how to help. I know how

because I've been through it, albeit on a different level. I've researched physical abuse though and where to go. Maybe that's why I was so caught up. Why I stayed. It could've been because I said it was not that bad," Pauline said.

"Men." Monica turned her head and stared, glinting her eyes at Pauline, almost trying to see more.

"I knew to leave, but I couldn't. Years and years it dragged on. For my daughter, for the life we had on the surface, for our friends, it was the only way to continue. I didn't want to jostle or disrupt anything in the picture-perfect world."

"Me too," Monica said.

They both sat quietly.

"You know I had all these bruises. Sometimes he would hit me in spots that were inconspicuous just so I wouldn't have to explain it to my friends. That was his kindness. All that time, I said it was better than someone's couch. Better than losing my job for not having an address. Better than sleeping in a shelter. The words, 'they won't understand,' resonated in my mind every day." Monica patted her fist on her thigh. "I was afraid of the unknown."

The first night on the road, the ladies took separate rooms. Pauline was happy to pay for both. It was more of a motel off the side of the road at the top of Massachusetts. They hadn't planned it, as Tera would have. Tera would certainly disapprove either way.

They had figured the girls would call around dinner time because they didn't call immediately. Pauline had been right that the girls continued on by themselves, likely embarrassed by their behavior. They sipped wine at all fourteen planned wineries and then returned home. The house was empty house. Luggage could only be found in one room, their own.

They likely freaked out. Pauline had called that as well.

When they called, the first three times, Pauline and Monica were still driving. They didn't want to talk just yet. So, as they continued to call, the two continued to drive, persistent, convinced they would turn around if they answered. The top was down; they said this to each other.

After they paid for the room and settled in, they called together.

"What are you doing;" "where did you go;" and "really, it was hard to plan this vacation;" were all questions that spouted loudly through the telephone one speaker, somewhere in upstate New York. Tera sounded livid. Her attitude really could flip with a switch.

"Girls, girls. It's my fault. I'll take the grounding when we get home. But my friend is in trouble. She really said she needed out and I must help. It's not fair the lot everyone has in life. We have a chance to save her before something worse happens. Isn't that worth it? I'm not putting Monica in danger, but she is invaluable to me. I couldn't do this alone."

"We bought steaks, Mom. To apologize. Steaks. The good cut. Not ground chuck for burgers, right? Mom, if you turn around now, you could be home in several hours."

"Nope dear. We are on a journey. We will help this woman in distress." Pauline winked at Monica. "If this is the only thing I've ever taught you…It's helping people. Be selfless now and again. Don't you think you could do that, Tera?" Pauline asked.

There was still silence. The only sound was the noise of the wind rattling against the glass motel window.

"Mom, are you okay? Is Pauline holding you hostage?" She adjusted the phone. "Ow," Casey said.

"Yes. Everything is fine. I'm okay. I wanted to do this."

"We'll just be gone for a few days. That's all dear," Pauline said.

"Jesus." In the distance, moaned words called out. All three traced the grunt to Tera. "Be safe." The words came across as yelled from a distance on the other side of the phone.

When they returned to their separate rooms, Monica lingered in the doorway. "Are you sure you're all right?"

"Yeah. I'm fine. You ever gone through a mid-life crisis?"

"No. I guess not."

"I can count five on my hands." Pauline chuckled. "I guess

some people were just meant to keep searching for more, something different, something new."

"You'll be all right."

"I know I will."

Pauline sat cross-legged on the floor, not wanting to stream her exercise class, merely thinking about her run through her yoga poses, and avoiding arranging her clothes for the next day. She laid the backs of her palms on her knees and just was. She tried to find her center, breathed in and out, as someone had told her to do in a class. That same class she watched every day. That was the problem. She always listened and did. Never had the spark, the urge. Never acted on impulse. Told and do. That was the story of her life. Here she was of her own accord. Going into the depths of Maine for something she genuinely believed in and believed could be.

She left her phone on in case one of the girls would call her in the middle of the night, have an emergency, make her reveal her whereabouts, or make them come home. If they begged, she might have come home. But they didn't beg. Once you say the word abuse to a twenty-something, they stop in their tracks. That's what Pauline had done. Stop them, for better or worse.

Pauline's dad had gotten sick again that week. Tera wasn't told. She didn't want to ruin the vacation. She hoped not to cause too much heartache. Or awkwardness even with Monica and Casey. Tera would've cried. She would've been down in the dumps. She would be as soon as Pauline told her.

She paged through a medical dictionary she had brought with her. They said it was a drug interaction that slowed him down, put him in the hospital, and it was something she didn't quite know about. So, she leafed through the medical dictionary looking up words she could've just as easily looked up on her phone. She guessed she brought it because it would be a Segway, a way to tell Tera the truth, an intro for disheartening news that must come out.

It was true, Pauline had not much liked her father. She remembered only his alcoholism growing up, and that trauma stuck. Pauline couldn't remember memories Tera spoke about when she was young; she only retracted into the powerful images. Despite the trauma he inflicted, that Pauline realized, she continued to see him, attached by blood. That simple reason and the reason that Tera seemed to love him. From what she could tell, they got along.

She had said send her his ashes. She had not gone down to see the body. They sat on the mantel delivered two weeks ago to the day. She hadn't much liked men or trusted them, at the very least, her whole life. Years ago, she divorced her husband. A two-timing asshole were the words that popped into her head every time someone mentioned his name.

She tucked herself in bed and raised her arm straight in the air like she had when Tera was young, four or five. Tera would not want to go to sleep, so when Pauline was lying beside her in her bed after a story, they would raise their arms to the air and hold them there. As soon as they fell asleep, they would wake up and readjust. Or it would fall and make a commotion. Tera would wake up. No matter how fun the game was, when Tera eventually tired of the game, when it was too hard to balance her arm, she would place it at her side and blissfully drift off to sleep. Pauline would tuck the cover under her chin to make sure she really was asleep and would flip out the small lamp at the bedside. She would pick up the book and place it somewhere to be found in the morning. This was their ritual. This is what Pauline would always remember.

She could swear she lost consciousness only out cold for minutes. When her eyes opened, bright light cascaded into the room, onto a spot just before her head. She turned her head into it and the warmth and the light stung her eyes. She was awake, and this happened to be a new day. The day would leave her with a new outlook on life. Once again, she had altered her life. She had done it at least three times before.

The first husband was short-lived. He was so sweet. Instead of abuse, he was a pushover. Pauline, in a way, took advantage of that fact. She tapped her foot if he didn't bring home flowers every day. She made him cook. He always paid for dates. Pauline was on top.

This was what she learned from her dad. She applied it in her first real relationship. Almost seeking out a pushover to control. She wanted to be in charge, the pusher. When she moved to his place, it was a major step. She changed her life for him. They got engaged and Pauline planned a wedding.

It was in this new row house downtown where they were socialites a bit. Out and about, they mingled with others that had a good position in life. Meanwhile, behind the closed doors, her to-be husband was finally satisfied. He got what he wanted, and the chase was over. He didn't do the dishes anymore, let alone cook. In true form, he trampled over Pauline's emotions. He had the gall to fart in the same room without pause. It was tears, tears, tears for Pauline.

Once Pauline lost control, she became quickly vulnerable. She swore it was that she bore her emotions, cried, and bared all that was the demise of the relationship. She could've gotten back on top. With tears, she went into detail about her father, his abuse, and how he made her weak. Her fiancée was unresponsive. He let her grovel even at his feet. Enjoyed it.

They got married and soon after Pauline moved out. She was a prize. The light at the end of the tunnel finally reached, and he didn't need her anymore. She took another place, started her life over again. Half the friends went to her. Half of the meager saving was donated by her ex-husband. She couldn't bear to argue over it.

Her life had cascaded and then come full stop, and she shut off. She knew she did. She wouldn't open her emotions to anyone ever again. With the sign of the cross, she swore to herself and on any prospective partner.

CHAPTER 18

Pauline rummaged around the room, getting her bags ready. The popcorn ceiling seemed to be shedding, and a few white plaster crumbs dirtied the bedspread she had loosely put back into place. She hoped she hadn't swallowed any bits while she slept. The picture of the beach and seashells on the wall were quite out of character, but she adjusted them nonetheless. A water spot lurked in the carpet's corner. She was unsure if the motel would charge her for any of the damage to the room.

Pauline brushed her teeth and flushed out the residue with a cup of water. It was such a rundown motel to have taken Monica to, and Pauline regretted it. She didn't have the wherewithal to find something decent under all the stress. Monica and Pauline had been excited, two women on an adventure, broken free from their daughters, from the world. But Pauline knew doubt lurked in Monica's thoughts. She just hadn't spent enough time with Pauline yet. Monica just wasn't as excited driving about with Pauline. She might not make it the entire way. But what would Pauline do? Put her on a bus, she guessed.

Throwing her bags in through the back door, Pauline locked it and made her way to a quiet 1950s restaurant by the hotel. What she wouldn't have given for a porter. Her arms ached, and she was stiff in the joints from a hard mattress. In the tiny shop next to the diner connected to the hotel, she found a road map, folded and stiff from age, from sitting on the turning rack by the register. It smelled of smoke, as the shop did.

She caught the eyes of a tall middle-aged man, certainly younger than Pauline, but old enough to be a friend. He reminded her of someone she was quite fond of when she was married to her ex-husband. "But, then again," she thought, "the relationship turned sour." He was only interested in her for what she had, and when her husband left and she was poor, or very thrifty at least, for several months, he removed himself from the friendship. "What a prick," Pauline said. She mumbled to herself in some other time or place.

Pauline met Monica at the entrance to the diner at just past 8:30 a.m. like they had planned. They both agreed that yesterday had been stressful, and they had needed an extra few minutes of sleep and relaxation. They were on vacation regardless.

Monica was already sitting just around the corner from a 1950s jukebox. It was the highlight of the diner, an otherwise run-down relic, not maintained quite enough to be gimmicky as a 1950s diner.

Pauline had something to say between long sips of coffee. After each sip, she held the mug just away from her mouth and she felt a gap form between her lips. Words did not issue. She thought better of herself and pulled the mug right back to her lips.

"I can't believe we're doing this." Monica's eyes drooped. "I hardly slept."

"This is an adventure. You'll sleep better tonight. You...You don't know how much this means to me, Monica. Really, you don't. I wouldn't be able to do this myself."

Pauline unfolded a traditional roadway map like they were back when the diner first opened, planning a trip like a couple on vacation. "I think we'll get to Vermont by the end of the day. We'll have a few stops, but it should be a pleasant day."

"Time is of the essence, though. Right Pauline?"

"Of course, of course. But she isn't expecting me until Friday."

"Right, this might be longer of a trip."

"How are you young ladies doing? Did you like your meal?" The man put his arm across the back of the booth seat and leaned in on Monica.

Pauline quickly shifted directions, and half turned her

back to the man, examining the map. "Oh, we're fine." She flitted her hand away from her in an attempt to make him realize they didn't want to be bothered.

"Is that your speedy car out there, ma'am? It sure is nice," the man said.

The man was over six feet and had a scruffy, uneven beard. Pauline could smell last night's booze.

"No," Pauline muttered.

Monica piped up, and a smile grew on her face from the attention. "What do you mean?" She giggled and twirled her hair. Monica obviously didn't smell the booze.

"Where are you ladies going?" He stepped back at her reception. "It looks like you're going to Maine. We're from Maine. Here for a car show, yup." He put his hands in his pockets and lifted onto his toes.

"We're going to Maine…ah, to visit a friend. We're making a stop in Meanderdon. I'm excited to see the shore."

"Really now? Would you want to come out to see a car show with me and my buddy today? Oh, please, before you leave?" He arched his back, and his untucked shirt pulled up past his belt, revealing rough hair on his stomach.

"Absolutely not." Pauline shrugged again and jerked back to her map.

"What Pauline means, sir, is that we don't have the time today." Monica winked.

"Let me give you my number…what's your name again?" the man asked.

"Monica," Pauline shouted.

"I'll give you my phone, Monica, and if you change your mind, we'll get together."

"Aww. We really don't live around here." Pauline cut off the conversation.

"Still, Monica here might want my number." He scrawled some digits on a napkin but didn't put a name on it and said goodbye casually. "You sure are beautiful, Monica. You take care now."

Monica blushed again.

"What's your favorite kind of car, Monica?" Pauline said.

"Why is that? I'm not sure, really. I guess I like Mitsubishi sports cars. They're nice. When I retire. Why? Why do you want to know?"

"Just small talk Monica. No real reason."

They gathered their belongings after they finished their eggs, and the third coffee was downed. "It's nice to be noticed by men is all, Pauline. You get it, what I mean?"

"Well, not as much lately," Pauline muttered to herself as she turned to scoop up her jacket.

"What's that?"

"That one just seemed creepy. That's all," Pauline said.

"I guess. But you really need to work on your wingman skills if we're going to be friends."

"Ok. I'll try. I promise."

Pauline walked confidently to the register to pay the bill and Monica called to Pauline that she would leave the tip on the table. She lingered at the table and flirted with the man who had sat back down. He pulled her to lean in, and she did.

Pauline looked away. She shouldn't judge. Monica stood on her own feet and made her own decisions. Monica certainly didn't act as prudish as Pauline. That's what she might think. Pauline was prudish, rude, and lacked sexuality, flirtation, desire. She would learn to loosen up. She must. Years with her husband had crushed her soul. As he tried to train her to be the wife he wanted, she eventually relented. When he made her repeat back the things he wanted her to say, they seeped in. When he dressed up for political events and work dinners, he had expectations, an air to keep, a persona to fulfill, words that must and must not be said, people to exclude and include. That's what her marriage was for years.

Here she was, unable to retrain herself, unable to bark commands at herself to restructure her mind. She could only hold on to Monica and hope she showed her how to be, how to be a woman with an opinion, appeal, appropriate but daring. Monica had all of those things, and she took chances. This was Pauline's chance to let it seep in and take a chance.

In fact, she had leaped to see Cathy. This was a major leap. She was a new person when they screeched out of the rental on route to fulfill a promise, a desire.

Pauline's same red car sat out front of the motel. It had gotten dirty and might need a run through a car wash. The mountain roads did it.

I tucked a single rose under the passenger side wiper. "Oh, Jesus Christ. Stalker…" Pauline said. She couldn't shake her gut's empty howl about this man, influence by her husband or not.

"I think it's cute," Monica said. "If we ever run into someone like him again, let's see where it goes. We are on an adventure. It's not only for you, is it?" Monica said.

"Monica, you are such a free spirit." Pauline looked Monica right in the eyes. "Two women together can be vulnerable. Let's just be careful," Pauline said. "I want you to understand, though, how good you are for me. How much you've changed me and influenced me. Your carefree ways will rub off, and I want that. I want to have your perspective, your energy and spunk." Pauline smiled because she meant it.

CHAPTER 19

The June heat singed the back of Pauline's neck. The car was open to the air again. Each time they took off, Pauline and Monica began it with a scream, a holler of freedom. No matter how unprompted or how low their spirits were, by the end of the holler it was a high-pitched squeal of excitement. This time was no different. They had taken off, wind blowing through their hair. They were back on the open road. The moving air was cool against the side of her neck and the beads of sweat that laid stale on her forehead. Monica put on a floppy beach hat to hold her hair tame in the wind. She was without a true compass and grew to embrace the unknown she was heading into.

"We're like sisters. However, you want to see it. I'm living a new life. I would never have. This is such a thing. Really," Monica said.

"Who's your best friend? I want to replace her." Pauline narrowed her eyes and leaned, looking forward at the road.

"Eileen. She's horrible." Monica laughed.

Monica and Pauline found they had a mutual friend. Eileen, she was just too blunt about everything. Monica swore she would never be friends with her again.

"I broke up with her. You know I'm free to friend date," Monica said. "She just, you know, talks about people behind their backs. She gossips and is chatty. For the first time in my life, I'm choosing to end a relationship."

"I know her." Pauline all but growled. "She's horrid. She talks about her friends like they're her enemies. I know what you mean. Years ago. This is years ago; I'll have you know. She told a mutual set of friends I had died. I went on a long vacation, that was really all. Can you believe it?"

"Totally something she'd do."

"I wasn't dead! She probably said it in just a way to lead to intrigue or to intimate I was as good as dead—a terrible friend."

"She's despicable. I know." Monica leaned in. "So, I cut it off. Like a child would say, 'I didn't want to see her anymore.' She flat out told me she would ruin me. I can't wait to see what she does. I don't even care. Because she is not around me. Won't be. I'm good."

"Listen, I'll take her place. I've known her for so long. I almost feel responsible. I'll tell you what she spreads around town, and we'll fix it. In the meantime, I'll be your best friend."

Monica held up her pinky finger and wrapped it around Pauline's. "We're too good to be true, Pauline."

"Too good. It's true."

This would be the longest day's drive. They would end up in northern New Hampshire, just outside the border of Maine. But Cathy didn't expect them for at least another two days. They had agreed upon it. That's what she told Monica this morning. Her name was Cathy, and she was just a great person. Too great to pass up.

This car, the getaway vehicle, was too much. It was a gift from her ex-husband. He gave it to her a few years ago as a final apology gift, as he put it. He supported Tera and Pauline while Tera grew up, and Pauline had also taken half. The car had a simple note. "I'm sorry. This is the only way I can say it." Pauline had taken it, begrudgingly at first, until it became a sign of liberation. Her choice was to say no to her ex, to not take him back. It became a choice she had made to accept or not accept. It was a symbol not of his apology but of her decision to allow him to fully leave.

"I'm gay!" Pauline yelled it into the wind. She turned her head partially away from Monica, so it wasn't a wonder that Monica didn't hear it clearly.

"What?" Monica shouted, a big grin on her face.

"I'm gay! We're going to see my would-be lover. Tell me I'm not losing it."

"What?" This time the voice was deep, low, with a stern face to match.

"Oh, boy. Here we go. Just wait a minute. I need to stop," Pauline said.

The car rumbled to a stop in a pull-off area. Pauline felt the coast of the car on loose gravel. She heard the loud pop of a few rocks that shot out from underneath the tires. Dust kicked up into the air and they both coughed. Monica pulled her shirt up over her mouth and nose, and Pauline covered her mouth with her hand.

"It's really…I'm gay." Pauline paused.

"Oh, Pauline. I am so happy for you. It changes nothing." Monica leaned over and hugged Pauline, still buckled into the driver's seat.

After that, they stared at each other, sharing blinking glances. Monica and Pauline were without any words. They both knew why they were going. It was clear as she screamed in the summer wind in a sports car with the top down. And still they had to talk about it.

"I met Cathy online after my ex-husband gave me this car. I felt so rejected when he gave it to me. He said we'd never get back together and that became the sever. It was a power move. It was a pity present when he finally got remarried. Albeit a much younger woman. I signed up for a divorcee support group online, probably much like yours, and I met Cathy, and she is just so. Magical, yes. Beautiful, yes. Spectacularly communicative, yes. She's just what I need. She dwells on contentious topics and looks at you with deep beady eyes when you should be listening. Her arms flail when she is irate about the world. She deepens my passion. I think…well…I might love her. I want to save her. When she tried to come out to her husband, he abused her. He, emotionally and financially, tried to hold her captive. When she told him about me, there were hundreds of threats. So, you see."

"This is all so much, Pauline. I really am happy for you." She shuddered, pulling in a deep breath and then relaxing into her seat.

"So, you can see. We developed a bond. She wanted me to come up for so long and I couldn't. It was so hard to make the commitment. I do care for her, but what if I don't feel 'it' when I see her in person? Love her, yes, of course. I think I do. But what if? I needed someone to come with me—"

"Of course. Of course, girl. We'll work it out. I'm here. Talk to me. We'll figure this mess, this beautiful relationship to come. Whatever it is out. I'm here for you."

"I'm not sure if I would have understood at first. I'm glad for setting things right before we got there, or I would've been even more confused."

They hugged again, and Monica kissed Pauline on the cheek. It showed her care, her concern.

Monica scrambled into the back and rummaged through her suitcase. She displaced pink makeup bags, lacey bras, and a thick rain slicker to get a rainbow pinwheel. "From the girls," she said.

Monica affixed the pinwheel to the rearview mirror. "You're out now. Might as well tell the world."

"But what if I don't…what if it doesn't—"

"You said you love her. It will all work out. Everything will be fine, be good."

They stopped at the next gas station at Monica's request. She needed a bathroom break. It was cooler, but the sun still shone down. Pauline stayed in the car and waited. She was glad for a break, but anxious about their next true destination and the last stop.

The women were reckless, and one might say, on the run. They looked twice at a police officer as he studied their car and their luggage as they entered the restaurant. He leaned in to look over the door and scratched the scruff on his chin. Monica's eyes raised.

When they returned to the car, before they left, they put their heads together and called the girls.

"Let's call the girls," Monica said.

"Ok. We really should, but we can't tell them about Cathy. About the rendezvous." Pauline added a lilt to the last word with emphasis being that the meetup was something special indeed.

"Ok. Stick to the plan. We're going to help an abused woman. The girls will believe it."

Pauline dialed on her phone. "Tera. Now, don't get upset. We're just checking in," Pauline said.

"Let me call Casey over," Tera said.

"What are you girls doing? How are you doing—" Monica said.

"Hold on." There was a pause. "We are doing the wine tours. Did you save your friend?" Tera said.

"Has to be the right day," Pauline said. "A few more days and all will be good," Tera's mom said.

"How are the wineries?" Pauline said.

"Great, great. Sans moms, the wineries are great."

"Are you two getting along?" Monica chimed in.

"Well, bring us some bottles home. I've got empty spots on my rack just for this event."

"Right. Moms be careful," Casey said in the distance.

"We will…" The four of them knew little what else to say. In half, the awkwardness broke them. The moms had left, leaving the girls in shock. The moms thought this was good in a way. So, they could work on themselves. Figure things out. If their relationship would not work, it was not viable. That was it.

Monica's hand fell to the leather seats. She rubbed it with light strokes. "I just hope they work it out." It was both their sentiments.

Pauline worried about her daughter off and on. One, she was an adult and starting what might be a relationship for the rest of her life. But Tera was young still and could call this relationship frivolous, not important in the long-term plan. Pauline tried to gauge the entire trip, which it was for Tera. Was she committed to the relationship and planning on marrying Casey, or would she dump and recover quickly as she had in her even younger year? Pauline could not quite tell which it was.

Pauline mused, sitting there in the parking lot, wondering what Monica was to her. Pauline could differentiate her status as Casey's mom from their own friendship that was growing. But what would Monica be like if their daughters broke up? Pauline wasn't sure. She would stretch to make their relationship solid on this short but important trip, so that she and Monica could still be friends after the breakup, if there was a breakup. Monica could be Samantha to her. They could be that close.

A strange tall man with a thick dark beard and dark hair flowing every way, thick and wily, brushed by the front headlights of Pauline's car. He looked straight ahead and did not engage, but Pauline stared. Pauline thought for a second that he might be homeless, in a cult, or just out of prison. His long jacket rubbed against the front headlights, and his demeanor said he was up to no good. His gait was fast, and he looked both ways before he entered the store. Pauline looked at Monica and knew she could only think what Pauline was—They should leave as quickly and quietly as they had come.

They did not egg on dangerous incidents, but they were following Pauline and Monica. Pauline closed her eyes and breathed to find a meditation point. But she knew she couldn't hold the silence and quiet. They must go.

When Pauline engaged the transmission into drive and skidded out, they were both back in it. A redirected purpose was anything but stifling. They both saw the trip with renewed vigor. It truly was a more joyous cause and Monica was fully in. Pauline needed nothing else, except maybe Cathy. To know more about Cathy and who she was in person, in the flesh.

CHAPTER 20

As they moved closer to their destination, their moods lightened, and they were excited to see the coast. The water in the Finger Lakes was nice, and if it was a little warmer, they could've swum, but the ocean was broad and open. Its impressive power was a sight to see.

"I love to just watch the waves crash," Monica said.

"Well, let's take a moment on the beach, gather some shells for the girls. We have all day. Cathy won't be ready for us until tomorrow. I just couldn't intrude."

Pauline's politeness was sometimes obnoxious. She couldn't barge in on Cathy a day early, though. She was working on a marketing freelance job and needed some time to complete it. Pauline didn't want to be a hassle that showed up at her door. Pauline inhaled the salty air.

"Do you hear that, Monica? The coast. It's rejuvenating," Pauline said.

"Absolutely. And, yes, let's stop and run the sand on our toes. That's what I most want to do here."

They slowed into a pull-off close to a long pier filled with bustling businesses and tourists. People who hadn't time to spend any other way. They basked in the gluttony of shopping and a fine day. Pauline was silent and Monica didn't ask questions. They both knew with a nod they must go out toward the water on this beach, the coast they had finally found.

The day warmed with the reckoning sun, despite how far north they were. A cool air chilled the tiny hairs on Pauline's forearms. When she looked up to the sky, she should have felt the radiant warmth. Instead, all she could sense was the slight chill in the air that transferred to her body.

"Isn't this wonderful? This place, Meanderdon," Monica said.

They walked out onto a deep beach where no one dared to swim, even in late June. The opposite was true for the Finger Lakes. The girls had planned a swim day at a waterfall park near Ithaca. It would've been marvelous to cool off in the lower New York heat that must've just been raging. Here, though, they resigned themselves to walking on a beautiful beach without swimming. Pauline could've spent all day in a beach chair and never made her way in.

"Yes. Absolutely. And we're going to Portland tomorrow?"

"Yes. That's when Cathy is expecting us. I can't just show up unannounced. I'm sure she'd—She must work, but I'm sure. Jeeze, I haven't called her in several days. It's really going to surprise her. I hope she doesn't slam the door on me."

"Oh. I'm sure she couldn't ever…"

The two walked on the open shore, quick friends with a purpose in mind, a collaboration to get one what she wants. A traveler in a booth on the pier above them could give them no other fortune than a happy one, one that said someone destined them for a powerful friendship. One where each sacrificed for another at some point in their lives. They met mere weeks ago and had immediately bonded. This trip, this adventure that they were having, was so much about building their friendship, a friendship they knew they had to have, wanted to have.

Pauline strayed from Monica against the shoreline, shoeless toes wiggled in the sand. She ran up against the shoreline and then, when the water neared, she backpedaled to the safe, dry sand. Looking over her shoulder, she saw Monica tracing her path while sitting on the shore.

If this is all she did for the rest of her life, she could be happy, she thought. The ocean was like a voice she wanted to hear. It was the silence and the sound that she needed the whole time. It was the accompaniment to her loneliness she always needed. Of course, she liked Cathy's company, but she cherished her time alone as well. Cathy understood. While aloneness appeared sad at face value, some people needed to recharge. They needed to have that moment of reflection, that inward conversation to be. Sometimes they needed it to be with the world.

Picking up several pebbles, soon Pauline's pockets sagged down with her own runes, present telling stones of a memorable time. A vacation had. One was a shell, another smoother than any other she had found. The third was a lug of a rock of foreign origin. She would give each one to someone she was fond of back home: Tera, Casey, Robert. Instead of wine, this gift was simpler but also more profound. She dug a thought into each one that only a diamond could cut clearer. The rocky foreign object would go to Casey because she needed to apologize for Tera's behavior, for their mother and daughter's rocky relationship that had caused all the frustration. The shell would be Tera's because, in her opinion, and she would tell her as much, Tera should go slow like a turtle or mollusk, calm down, cover herself when a mom launched anxiety, created a fissure. As for the smooth rock, that one would be for Robert, because she had promised to smooth things over with his ex. She would follow through on the promise to make them friends.

Pauline chucked a few more back in the ocean because she couldn't find meaning, no matter how deep she investigated grooves or hardness. She ran along the shoreline, popped it into the water. This was her justice refilling the coastline like everyone does, some aware, some not of the impact. She removed two stones and two shells. She promised to bring three back when she returned with Cathy. They would cast them back in the same spot on a trip with all three of them together. They would see to it.

CHAPTER 21

It was 10:00 a.m. and early for Tera. She would go for this run. She would train, be better, be the person she always wanted to be. It was self-induced pressure, but she thrived on it. Would anyone really care if she sweated it out on this run? Doubtful, but she would know. She couldn't hide the lie from herself.

Casey lingered on the single couch in the living room. The book she was reading was thick, and the cover had muted colors for the illustration of a woman in a room reading a book. Swirls of art nouveau decoration accompanied the image. Tera liked the swirls, the decoration, better than the illustration, a woman in the center.

They were glad to have the place to themselves. And they were moving about in their own spaces. Separated from their usual codependence, they did not fight every second. Maybe this was what married life was like, finding space to breathe and do your own thing. Dating was so intense. If you were around your partner, you were stuck with all the emotions, stress, and behaviors. I guess in most relationships, that's where the break was. There was only so much nose picking or annoying laugh or pressure to make more money before someone cracked. You were too much in that person's space. It was the ones who made it to marriage; she guessed that relaxed into their own space, found pause. Time away from the laugh. Moved to the bathroom to pick a nose. Casey was also free to do whatever she wanted without being totally attached to Tera. Tera relished her self-imposed independence.

Tera swung her hips as she moved into the yard. The dogs, those killer dogs, were gone. They weren't the only terror in this small town, though. There was a junkyard just down the road. How unsightly it was. She was apprehensive about a plan to even get to the town. She'd have to run on the road for some bit before she got to sidewalks. There was only a narrow berm. She had promised to pick up some extra biscotti from the bakery. She must make it to town.

Still, she lingered in the driveway. The driveway with no car. They decided that they'd Uber to a rental place today and pick something up for the rest of the week. They could afford it. It wasn't the issue. The stress of her mother leaving was the issue. The marked tantrum or childish reaction to her situation. She left. In the middle of their dual family vacation. Just left.

She touched her toes to loosen her back. A bead of sweat trickled down the side of her face in the sun, now arching on its way across the sky. She lunged left and then right. Then put her front leg in front of her, stretching. "If you're not into yoga…" Tera sang at the level of a whisper.

"Why are you so blocked?" Casey had said.

Tera was blocked. She knew it. She had to keep up appearances. She knew Casey wouldn't love her if she opened it. It ate at her, and she knew it. Not being able to share. Only being able to reject what she once was. What would her boss say? Her friends? She was just not out in the open and she was used to it. What she made herself into, perfect body, perfect image, was everything. If she opened up, she would lose it. She knew it for sure.

Cars sped by her, leaving a sizeable gap. She guessed that the New York state drivers would be a little more kind, and they were. This place was so laid back and there were so many vacationers. She heard few if any city accents since she'd been there. A man rolled down his window minutes later as she was gaining confidence in her stride. "Get out of the road." New York City. Everyone from everywhere came from New York City.

Mark came from the city. Mrs. Calhorn and Mr. Calhorn attended college there. New York University. Mark wanted to return to the city until he disappeared. Tera never quite got over Mark. The steam of the sun on the blacktop was like her ritual shower after she finished a run. The steam felt like it lifted in a fog from her forehead. She imagined she walked in a mist of her own creation. Her own dreams formed. A cloud formed above her head and beads of rain reformed, drizzled.

Mark had left that night; the night they found the body at the bottom of the bridge. It was his best friend, one he often canceled with to go see Tera. Tera guessed he felt responsible. The relationship had gone much deeper than they ever would or could. He left that night with Tera's heart. Is that why she had rejected men because they had hurt her? Possibly, but not likely. When he touched the body, he got blood all over his hand. He kept saying they'd think he'd done it. He had Jason's blood on his hands.

When Mark called Tera down to the bridge that night, in the middle of the night, she'd just assumed that Mark had found him after he jumped. When she got there and saw him crouching at the base crying, she thought, she was sure.

Instead, he said they had both meant to jump, and he just hadn't. He felt he killed Jason that night because he couldn't do the act. Because they both didn't die, he was a murderer. He said this with conviction. He wailed at her the next day that he was a survivor but also a pusher, someone who didn't reach out his hand to bring him back on the bridge.

Tera wouldn't have told. She never told. But when they found the body two days later, after school had started back up on a Monday, Mark was gone. He took with it his innocence in a crime and the innocence of his childhood. Tera never told. She never covered it up. She said she hadn't seen him, didn't have any idea where he had gone.

When they couldn't find him, they went to her. She became quiet. She was seventeen and a few years of partying had taught her to be quiet. Mark's disappearance taught her to straighten up.

He didn't push Jason. She was sure of it. Tera covered nothing up; that much was true.

In a second, Tera would go back to Mark. When he surfaced again. She told herself that at eighteen and twenty-two, when she ran away to New York to look for him. That's where he'd run to, she had thought, where he'd have the most opportunity.

For all the years, she was with women; she was still in love with a man, a boy, she had known for two years. She panted and stopped as she found clarity. Something she rarely did. It was always push through it, pull more sweat. She stopped and put her hands on her knees and panted. The emotion of that night, of the partying too, and the rebellion. It bottled up in her and she would never sweat that out. She never wanted to be in a heterosexual relationship again, but maybe, if it was him, she could rekindle. For her mother. So, Samantha and Robert could be a family again. For them all to be together and go on a vacation together. Tera coughed out a laugh. It might be if they hadn't lost Jason if Mark hadn't left his life, too.

Tera walked it off in the driveway, always with a keen eye looking for the dogs. She found no reason to go in just yet. She had to shake the run, the visions of her last love off in the growing heat of the day.

Tera wasn't sure what they'd do that day. She wasn't sure if they'd interact or if she'd have the opportunity to fall into herself again and get lost in a past that haunted her so much. She shook her arms in waves.

Tera was glad they didn't need to get drunk to have a fun time but ached to go out and see people and put on a happier face. She felt she had to perform to get rid of these pervading thoughts, the ones that drift into your sleep and stick with you throughout the day.

Tera knew the only way she could shake it off sometimes was to be around people, to act in a way and be alive, to actually be alive. She would do that today in front of Casey or the bartender at the wineries.

Tera burst through the door with a big smile. "We're going to have a wonderful day, honey. I am confident about it. Lots of conversation, lots of alcohol, lots of sex," Tera said.

"All from this house, I hope. I don't want to go out," Casey responded.

"Of course, honey. All those same things. In the middle of the day, no less. With each other. Wouldn't have it any other way," Tera said.

Tera was performing. She was dancing like a free spirit so early in the morning to make things okay, to lift spirits and make things go on without the moms, without this rift she had created. The botched vacation Tera ruined with her words.

CHAPTER 22

They climbed a slight hill at the edge of the beach and moved up the road. Monica clasped Pauline as they scrambled on the rocks, taking her elbow in her arm and resting her hand on her back as they crawled up a section with large rocks. The pavement was warm and radiated onto their bodies and skin. They traversed up the road, just passed the line into a thin swath of gravel, hoping to not get hit. When they reached the top of the winding road, they sauntered up to the pier to see the ocean from up high, this magical place in Maine. They had veered off because Monica said she had always wanted to see this coastline. So, the car made a beeline just for Monica. They would see the ocean. Cathy second.

"Oh. The girls would like cotton candy. I can only imagine how they are. Do you think they've totally made up?" Monica held some shell jewelry in her hand and took out her wallet. "They'll need souvenirs at the very least to make up for our shenanigans." Monica pulled some ones from her wallet. A wad of ones, fives, and twenties protruded out of the center. They hadn't had to tip the winery staff because they hadn't even gone.

They stood next to a mock Viking ship, staring, not believing the vessel had landed up against the pier. The duo wouldn't have traded its majesty for stuck up wineries at that very moment. They were happy to just be where they were and be going where they were going.

Just then a voice chided, "Ahoy Mates!" A man with a scruffy beard but laundered and cared for clothing, a button down and khakis, and a woman with a butch haircut approached them. "Haven't seen you two around here often."

"Surely, you're not a pirate. Wait from the diner?" Monica chided.

The man was, in fact, the same man Monica had encountered in the diner. He had the same suave come-ons and half-cocked smile. He leaned in first, this time around, to Monica.

"No, ma'am…Just a sucker for tourists. And yes, from the diner. I live here. Serendipity it is. I'm originally from a town just north of here, but I've set up roots here for so long I've gotten a tattoo." He pulled up his t-shirt sleeve and bared his arm that held a scrawled "Meanderdon." It was an armband, of sorts. She could see more words, another arm band, above his sleeve but didn't pry.

"Hi. How are you?" The woman bobbed her head down as she approached, appearing to be mostly speaking to Pauline.

"Can we take you fine ladies out for a seafood dinner? Our treat," Mike said.

"We need to discuss." Pauline whipped Monica around and made for a corner beside a booth with a curtain hanging over it. "Monica, I get it. You're on the prowl, but really? These two?"

"Why not? It's harmless. It reminds me of my teens at the beach when guys would simply go up and ask you out. Come on. It'll be fun. Then we'll go see Cathy in the morning," Monica said.

"My god what I get myself into. It's fishy—Are you sure? My god. Is this ever more than an adventure?" Pauline said.

Pauline sauntered back over to the two strangers and offered them her hand. "Hi. I'm Pauline. I'm used to knowing someone's name before they take me to dinner."

"Uh. Mike. Mike. Nice to meet you and…" His eyes extended over to Monica, and his eyebrows raised.

"Monica. Just Monica."

"This is Julie, Monica. It's my sincerest pleasure to introduce you," Mike said. He motioned with a bow.

"Hiya. I'm just along for the ride," Julie said.

"My daughter would kill me…" Pauline said as she got in Mike's car. Monica hovered outside the other passenger door, not ready to get in. She left her hand on the handle and froze.

"It's okay ladies. If anything happens, I know the police. In a few towns, I know the police. I'm one of those guys who donates to the force and brings donuts when something happens in his town, my town," Mike said. He laughed holding his belly.

"Oh, you know the police," Pauline said. "Who polices you?"

"Oh, I don't have a wife yet, right now at least, but there are people who look out for me. Is that what you mean?" Mike asked as he dashed around the car.

Mike hustled to open the door for Monica. "M'lady."

"Where are you ladies from?" Mike asked as he put the car in drive.

"Oh. I'm from Oregon, Pennsylvania," Monica said.

"Really. What brings you up here?" Mike asked another question.

"A friend. A friend of ours is asking for us in northern Maine," Monica said.

"What town?" His direct words seemed to grab rather than coax out an answer.

"We don't really need to share our plans, do we?" Pauline asked.

He didn't quit. "What town?"

"Selliesville," Monica said.

Pauline glared.

"What?" she said as she glared back into Pauline's eyes. She shrugged her shoulders and let her arms fall. "This will all be fun," she said and turned to pat her shoulder.

"I'm familiar. Yes. Remarkably familiar. You wouldn't know Cathy?" Mike popped open the can.

"Might…might know her," Monica said.

"Hush Monica—" Pauline cut her words.

"Thought you might," Mike said.

"Who do you know?" Pauline queried.

"Oh, no one. Never mind. Everyone is friends with a Cathy…" He gave a hearty laugh and quickly changed the topic.

Pauline was more than nervous. This character was prying into their lives, and he already had answers. This suspiciousness rolled with her stomach. What would she tell her daughter in this situation? If she were at the top of a mountain in a car with a boy, she'd have to walk all the way home. That's just how it was in the late seventies.

When they exited the car, Mike opened both their doors. Despite his suspiciousness, the chivalry was admirable. Pauline, and she gauged Monica as well, was almost getting used to the m'lady bit.

They entered the seafood shack, and there were beers all around. Soon they were swigging their drinks like they drank them in favor of wine. "Winery swinery," Pauline said before she gave a light burp.

Pauline felt like she was sixteen again, despite being in her fifties. While Mike pulled out Monica's chair, Julie pulled out Pauline's. Pauline accepted the sentiment willingly. It gave her a buzz like no other and she felt her head spin as she wondered what to say, tried to spit out words. Instead, she just sat down and relaxed, glancing at Julie and smiling in thanks.

They ordered lobsters all around. Monica spoke up. She couldn't believe how cheap they were. Despite this, Mike said of course he'd pay because he had friends on the staff. Mike and Monica exchanged several glances, and Pauline could tell her heart was off racing. Pauline sobered up to remember she wasn't a teenager, and this wasn't the savoriest moment she'd ever been in. But she was so happy to see Monica being wooed. She couldn't stop it. It would've devastated her. All she wanted was to have some attention.

When Mike asked Monica if she'd like to go for a walk on the beach and promised to be a gentleman, Monica consented. They picked up their things and sauntered out the back door to have supposedly have some quiet time next to the peacefully roaring water. Pauline and Julie stayed behind to pick at their food and then pack up the leftovers. Mike promised to have Monica back soon.

Soon Pauline became entranced even further by Julie's

heavenly stares and suave words. She said things like, "How can you be so beautiful and so free?" And "Why don't you live here? You certainly don't live here, but you should." The sentiments gave her a similar rise as the ones Cathy had spoken to her in the beginning. The words that wooed her and made her so star-crossed. It truly was a lesbian life that Pauline lusted for. These women were so enraptured. They gave so much of themselves. They cared. She couldn't think of anything else.

Pauline might've let Julie take her back to the car. They might've made out like teenagers. Pauline's lust might've rubbed off on the upholstery. But Julie hadn't asked, and Pauline thought about Cathy, how Julie was so much like Cathy in every word. Pauline would do anything to find her goal and she told herself Julie was just a weigh station, a minute of conflict and second thoughts. Her passion for a year awaited her in northern Maine, just north of here. Just tomorrow.

A loud clap came across the restaurant, and people shuffled but then relaxed back into their spot. Pauline looked nervous and tapped her fingers repeatedly on the table.

"Did that come from the beach?"

"Uh. Might've. Look beautiful, I might have to go. It's not that I don't want to tell you how beautiful you are and be with you, because I really do. I've loved our conversations. I didn't think—See, Mike wasn't supposed to go down to the beach—He's not always appropriate." Julie rose and walked toward the door. "The bills been paid." The restaurant staff did not approach when Pauline moved to follow Julie to the door. "They are. They are down at the beach," Julie said before she took off running.

Monica came leaping into the parking lot. "We've got to go. The car, your car, is just passed down the road. I don't get why we even drove for five minutes anywhere with those two."

"Did you?"

"I shot him." Monica raised her arms and let them cascade to her side. She breathed heavy breaths.

"Oh god. Monica!" The last word turned into a yell.

They took off running as fast as they could in the espadrilles.

They called back and forth to each other.

"He grabbed me. He wouldn't let me go. Oh, my god. They're going to think it wasn't warranted. We can't go to the police now. Can we? Will they believe us?"

"Oh, God, Monica. I should've never let you." They bobbed here and there on the skinny path just off the road in the dark. They panted and sweated and could barely see a thing in the deep black. Only a few stars were visible, and Pauline guessed it might rain.

"He had a gun. You ever learn that move where you grab someone's wrists and knee them in the groin. I learned it in gym class." Monica panted and slowed to a walk. "I'm glad I used it."

Pauline stopped and grabbed Monica in an embrace. "I'm so sorry. This is all my fault."

"Pauline, I am all too aware. I've had to fight off people before."

"Are we running from the police or Mike? That's all I need to understand."

"It grazed his arm. It's nothing other than self-defense. I'm running from Mike."

"Great. We need to get out of here."

They shuffled as quickly as they could down the road, staying outside the line in a thin strip. Pauline felt what could've been Mike's breath on the back of her neck and hurried a bit more quickly. Her bum ankle was aching.

This had been that late night encounter at the top of the hill. It was what she had wished she had done that night. Got out of the car. She shook herself a bit. She had let that boy take advantage of it. Here she was in the pitch dark, running from a man who violated her friend, and it was still trauma. She could never run away from that, but she could make it to their car. She could've made it down the hill.

When they reached the car, they chucked their shoes in the back seat and rubbed their blistered feet before Pauline turned the key to start up the car. She looked at Monica. "Are we really doing this running?"

"Yes. At the very least, it was self-defense." Pauline put her hands on the wheel and rolled them on the leather like a motorcycle.

They were both in the muck of it. Either way, they understood that man had committed a crime, and it was not their faults. But there was blood. There was blood on Monica and Pauline, too. Pauline had taken Monica in her arms, redirected her fear into Pauline's firm and quick acceptance of what had happened. It was not Monica's fault. Monica hadn't yet. It was Pauline's job to prove it.

"Monica, we don't have to talk about this, but it wasn't your fault. That man is evil. He deserves years in prison," Pauline said.

"Oh. It's just what good…" The response to her own statement had bellowed from her mouth before.

"This place. It's foreign. I don't want to create something that's not resolvable for weeks or months. Something that requires me to stay in this state when I just want to go home. I mean, after we see Cathy. Of course, after Cathy," Monica said.

"It's up to you, Monica. It's your decision." Pauline withdrew because she really didn't understand.

CHAPTER 23

They sat in the rental car, Casey in the driver's seat, headed dead southeast back toward home. That's the only thing Tera was sure of. Casey had been tight-lipped all morning. She had command in her voice. Good morning. Good morning. This is what she needed. They did that. Eat your eggs. She almost did. We are leaving. Tera packed her bags.

They locked the rental up, and Casey made a comment about opening up emotionally for the ride. Tera needed to open up, or they would never get anywhere. Casey could never break the brick wall Tera had created.

They left the place in the same condition they found it, run down, gross, with rust and mold as it may be. They pulled the comforters roughly over the beds as a courtesy, not fully making the beds, so the cleaners, or the owners, knew they slept there. "Not that it matters," Tera quipped. She tried to make light of everything that morning. Not even a shallow laugh.

Tera took out the trash, something she did regularly at home. They had made it her task. They put the dishes in the dishwasher. They turned it on and dropped the key in the metal lock box on the way out. It was ugly just like the place, a necessity, the same as the location.

They hadn't made memories here. They didn't have happy moments to look back on. Casey had taken a few photos of people smiling, but they were nothing to laugh about after the fact. In one photo, Pauline jabbed Tera repeatedly in the ribs until she smiled. A half-cocked grin lingered as her eyes looked down at her side.

"Casey. Is this right?" Tera asked.

"It's as right as it will ever be," Casey said. "We're just not ready for vacation together with moms, for vacation together, or even living together. We tried it and it was our demise." Casey smiled a full genuine smile, relaxed as she realized. "We can be civil."

"Of course, nothing but." Tera tried to force a smile, but the ends curled up irregularly.

"What was it, Casey? What made you decide? Why are we on this journey home?"

"Really Tera. It's the way you are so uptight. Nothing is ever perfect. Will I ever be perfect?"

"Oh, hon—" Tera stuttered.

"And what is up with you and your mom?"

"I was a bad kid. Me and my mom were rocky. Tera smiled impishly and looked up. We were always rocky since I was a teenager."

"Come on Tera. Everyone's been through a divorce." Casey took control of the wheel like she'd never been more confident, and it scared Tera. That this time it might really be done. They would not get a refund for the several nights left on the rental.

Casey had made breakfast that morning. The previous day, they stayed in their own bubble. Tera was sure that's what they needed, a break. But Casey, after she served the eggs, said. "No discussion. I want to go home. And you're moving out when we get home."

Enough said. Tera couldn't finish her eggs and teetered entirely off base. She could barely choke down her coffee. Even though she missed her mug that Casey had got her, that said, "Don't talk to me. It's morning." She wanted to be in bliss with Casey. And Casey was right. It just wasn't happening.

"Maybe I'm too emotional for women? Women can't handle me," Tera thought.

"I had this friend. When I was fifteen. Up unto…oh, I guess seventeen. He was a boyfriend, but not really. We fooled around but were friends first. Spent all our time together. We were so relaxed," Tera said.

Tera could be bisexual. She had never found someone she adored quite like Mark, her first crush. She couldn't ever expect another man to be quite like him. And at the same time, she longed for him like she had pined for him before, and the maleness that came along with him, at least once a week. If that made her attracted to men, then so be it. If the man before her was a perfect likeness to Mark, she would test the waters.

Here, with Casey in the same car as her, she whispered to herself that she would see what would happen. She would leave Casey to find peace.

"Why are you telling me this?" Casey's face now looked terrified.

"Because with me and my mom. We fought about him. Fought about the trouble I got into."

Tera wasn't sure whether if at that point in her life she loved Mark because her mom hated him or not, but she knew now, as she tried to repair the relationship with her mom, that she would love him forever. She could never…and this might be the last try…to find someone to relax with.

"Every kid fights with their mom."

"I just have the guilt, I guess," Tera said and paused. "We got into trouble, I guess. We stole candy bars. I got in trouble for skipping school too many times. He really was a bad influence. My mom was a single mom, and I gave her so much heartburn, heartache."

"You know this is part of the reason. It's why we won't work. Your surly past. Live up to it at least, but I can't believe you hiding. That's what's so unattractive."

Tera spit it all out then. The daily shenanigans. That time, they dumped water on a bum. "Oh, that was true to form," Tera said. "We told ourselves that we were doing a justice to society. We were helping clean up the streets." Tera was bold and unembarrassed as she talked. She didn't care if Casey never wanted to see her again. "At least it wasn't freezing cold. It was the summer. He probably liked it."

"I'm sure he didn't," Casey said.

"It was all wholesome fun. We didn't rob him or set him on fire like someone had done the previous year to a group of homeless people in tents down by the river."

"How can you be so proud of this?"

"That's just how we were. And I really cared about him, and I am proud of the fun we had. Ashamed, yes, but proud of the power we had together. That sensation I'll never shake," Tera said.

After a deep breath, she continued to talk about that time they stuck a knife in a teacher's textbook copy right before class. "He came into class and was awestruck. Oh, we got sent to the principal. We got Saturday detention because Jake saw us do it from outside the classroom before the door opened." Tera paused and folded her hands. "We got in big trouble, but we still got A's the rest of the semester. I don't understand how? We denied it all the way. Never held firmer to a lie until now."

"So anyway, then we did drugs with the janitor on Saturday detention. His weed was bad. It was horrible, dry, and brittle, but we smoked it and got a little high. No one caught us that time," Tera said. Her hand brushed back her hair, and she held them tight to her head.

"Then there was the bomb threat. We called it in, so we'd miss a test I hadn't studied for. To be fair, I probably would've passed, anyway."

Tera relayed incident after incident until Casey loudly said, "Stop." Casey pounded her fists on the wheel.

Tera needed to calm down her manic recounting of stories. She had to push small breaths out of pursed lips.

"Wait. But you must hear this." Tera smacked her lips. "Then he killed someone." Tera paused for effect. "Mark. Not me." She backed off.

"Do I need to get out of this car? I don't think I can do this, Tera. Who are you? What did you do?"

"I mean." Tears welled in Tera's eyes. "I loved him. I think I still do. Can you be in love with someone who is so foreign, who you never really knew?"

Casey put her eyes straight forward and stepped on the gas. "You know…" Casey scratched her cheek. "I can't do this."

They spent miles in silence. Tera knew she had said too much. She knew she couldn't convince Casey of anything. Casey likely didn't even care to hear her story. Someone died, and she didn't care. She said she didn't want to hear it. Tera herself covered up a murder and Casey could have given two shits. This day, this vacation, this life…

Casey dropped Tera off at her mom's house before circling back to their apartment. "Come by later, when I'm not there," Casey said. She turned on the AC a little higher and Tera looked back at her from the passenger seat.

"You drove all that way."

"I'm sweating. And yes. You didn't even offer." Casey turned to adjust her left vent. "So selfish," she muttered.

CHAPTER 24

They sat in the car panting, their heads rested back. Pauline was stunned they were safe. It was all Pauline could do but to lean her head back on the headrest and point her eyes at the ceiling. The two of them looked up, and Pauline noticed the blackness of the car ceiling and the ridges where the soft top crinkled.

"He said he was friends with the police," Monica said.

"I know," Pauline said. "Oh dear, I know."

They both sat breathless, staring out at the blackness before them, a sea of darkness that descended them into a black hole. Pauline shut her eyes.

"Monica?" Pauline started while both their heads still rested back.

"Yes, Pauline?" Monica responded.

"Can we just sit here longer? I'd just like for my brain to catch up with my breath."

"Absolutely, Pauline," Monica said. "What do you want for breakfast tomorrow?"

"What?" And then Pauline got it. "Eggs; hash browns or tater tots. I love when you can sub tater tots. I see a diner in our future. An all-night diner."

"Right. How about in an hour?" Monica asked. "Let's get a bit away from here if we can."

"Monica?" Pauline asked.

"Yes, Pauline?" Monica responded.

"When we go into the diner. Can we check to see if anyone has guns? I mean, can we scope the place out?"

"Absolutely. Why don't we both go to the restroom and then go back to the host's desk? Or I can hit the bathroom and return straight-away to the car?" Monica turned her head to look at Pauline's still resting face up.

"Both to the bathroom. Let's do that."

When Pauline's phone rang, she thought it could be one of three people: Tera, Robert, or Cathy. Monica probably only thought it was the girls checking in. When Monica told her to take it, Pauline reluctantly looked down and saw it was Tera.

"Hello," Pauline whispered a stern greeting. "Tera, this is just not the time," Pauline said.

"You have to come home, Mom. It's not right," Tera said. "You can't be with the enemy."

"What enemy. Listen, we—" Pauline covered the phone and cowered next to the door. "We are friends. That won't change. Not now after this trip."

"But Casey. She's horrible. It would not work. Right? We talked about it a bit. That it was not likely to work."

"Enough. Casey's mom is right here."

"Mom, come home." Tera whined one last plea.

Then Pauline hung up. She couldn't. She didn't have the patience this late at night with all that had just happened. Tera, when she was a child just like now, always looked after herself. She never thought of the other people in her life, what could be, and how to fix things. Pauline would help when she got home but now was not the time.

Here, Pauline had taken to liking women after Tera had been out for ten years. Tera came out early and often. Anyone she saw, she told, it seemed to Pauline. Pauline herself had feelings for women for a long time, but never like the painful want she had when she talked to Cathy. Cathy meant everything and had truly created an imaginary space for her, away from what she thought about sexuality because of her daughter. Cathy introduced her to another world, a world of older women who were doing things for themselves. They were finding themselves, being reborn. It was full of khaki shorts, just as much fine wine and cheese. Cathy promoted herself as a sophisticated woman and that was what Pauline had always desired. It was worth her whole life to move forward. Tomorrow was Day 1.

When Tera called, it reminded her of a failed relationship.

It reminded her that even lesbian relationships fail. Pauline had never even met Cathy, let alone felt her touch. She might fail, and then what. She would have to go back to New York with her tail between her legs. A lot of pent-up nervousness hit with Tera's call. It drowned out the immediate need to contact the police to pull the stick out of park and drive.

Monica heard. "What was that all about?"

"I didn't want to tell you, but Tera just called and said she and Casey broke up."

"Oh, is that all? They break up every other week."

"I, I didn't know."

"Casey tells me that's typical in a young lesbian relationship. I believe her."

"So, we can continue? On our trip? You don't want to go directly home?"

"Well, I almost got sexually assaulted. I must report it. Enough rapists in the world. You must take me to the police. We should go tonight. We are not getting out of the trip tonight. Oh, and yes…I still want to finish the trip with you."

"Oh, of course. Let's get you to the police station."

Pauline stared out at the water one more time. The place where they had searched for shells and meaning this morning was now covered over with tide. The way the sand felt in her toes, the freedom she had, what she had never felt as an adult, coursed through her veins for a moment more. Then she brought herself back to reality. Her passenger was the victim of a crime, and she needed to report it.

They trailed down the road, passing quickly by the seafood restaurant. Pauline remembered the taste of the butter and savory richness of the lobster. Monica had likely put it out of her mind already. Remembrances of unwanted advances probably overtook her thoughts.

"Monica?"

"Yes? Do you think any of us can ever be loved?" Pauline said.

"Yes. Love is out there. I believe. We just must cultivate it. We may find it by seeking it or letting events unfold in front of us. Either way, it's there. You just must look."

The sign, Mike, Julie, and the Lobster Shack hung in Pauline's mind. A plastic square with stylized text lit up the front of the building. Surely no one could shoot anyone right out front, abducted right out front. Unless it was Mike himself doing the abducting. Pauline didn't mention the sign name, didn't want to bank on her hunch about being right. She didn't want Monica to wake up from her desire to report the incident to the police.

They careened down the road. This time the streets were smaller and more winding, and the mood was something different. Pauline felt Monica heave a few sighs and saw her wipe her arm across her face out of the corner of her eyes.

"This Monica…is not so good." Pauline knew it wasn't. Pauline headed away from the diner. She wouldn't force and act, but she wanted it to be an option, not as much of a hurdle as it seemed looking out onto the dark beach. The vastness of the ocean had overwhelmed them. It had given a distinct pause than in the morning light. The darkness, the damp consuming ocean, enveloped. It ate them up.

"Monica, stay with me," Pauline said as she watched Monica dip her head in sadness or tiredness. Pauline wasn't sure. "Don't let yourself go." Pauline patted her own cheeks to show her she was trying to stay awake. She was sleepy, but she was staying awake for Monica. They would not pull over and take another break.

When they passed the lobster shack, Mike and Julie turned in unison toward the lighted sign. One part of on the lower left side of "Shack," the "Sh" and part of "a," flickered in the night's darkness. The dampness affected the lights; that saltwater ocean overpowered the land and the beach just as much. It devastated miles into the world. The pebbles Monica and Pauline would take back would resonate with the events, give the same amount of pause as they did on the beach in the car looking out. They would bring back the memories, the consuming ocean that swallowed them up. They got swallowed up in Maine. A townie named Mike ruined their trip.

CHAPTER 25

They pulled into the police station, still unsure what would happen. Monica had fired the shot. Her fingerprints were on the gun, too. She had blood on her clothes, albeit not a lot. They waited in the parking lot, and Pauline gave Monica the chance to speak. Pauline couldn't bring herself to say anything. When she did, it was a hushed statement that she was using a lifeline and calling a friend.

"He said he was in with the police, that's what he said," Monica said.

"That man who assaulted you, Monica, was a dangerous, evil man, yes. He knows the police, yes." They had discussed it on the way as well. "He traded favors or was a local buddy, yes. Monica, I don't know what to say. You have to trust the system. Report this."

"I can't chance a backlash when I file a report. I can't even chance them throwing the report away. It is humbling enough to have to go into the police station. I really am freer without the police. This precinct provides no sense of safety to me. The police will only pin it on me. I won't be able to handle that."

The police station gleamed blue and silver. A large line of cars stacked up against the side of the building and a door through which prisoners would exit the jail after a night over. A few seconds later, just as Pauline stared at it, an officer held the door open, and someone appeared. He looked left and right and stared right back at Pauline and Monica, sitting tight in the light of the parking lot. Pauline shuttered and her fingers dialed the digits.

"Samantha, I just didn't have any idea who to call. The girls would never understand." She made a quick pause that was not to be interrupted and spit out more words. "We were going to see Cathy. I told you about Cathy?"

Pauline kept certain things quiet, and even though Samantha was exploring her own sexuality with a woman, she still was tight-lipped. She didn't want to ruin Samantha's party; her coming out. So, she muted her own. She only mentioned a friend she was getting to know better. She might've been embarrassed.

"Cathy who? Oh, Pauline, you're so secretive. Is that the lesbian you mentioned twice, like three times? Why do you keep things so bottled up?"

"Yes. Yes. That's her."

"That's not real, is it?" Samantha said.

"This is why I didn't tell you, Samantha."

"I'm compassionate Pauline. I just wish you'd talk about it more. It seems so weird that you haven't met yet. Even for lesbians."

"Well, anyway, we are on this journey," Pauline said.

"Wait, aren't you supposed to be in the Finger Lakes with your daughters?"

"Well, we made our own trips. Girls were fighting. It was a lot." Pauline motioned Monica away, even though there was nowhere for Monica to go, when she talked about the girls, when the conversation got a bit more pointedly angry.

"What do you need, Pauline? This all sounds so baffling."

"We aren't quite in our senses, and we want to know if we should go to the police. A man assaulted Monica. We joined these two people for dinner and the one tried to take advantage of Monica."

"Oh my," Samantha said.

"That's not the worst of it. She shot him."

"Go in and report it. Yes. That's what you should do. Absolutely."

"It's a bit more complicated. Cathy mentioned to me he said her ex was investigating me. He had connections with the police." Monica was out of earshot.

"Oh no. Don't drag me into this. Robert and I just broke up. I don't want to live in fear." Samantha sniffed in a breath of air in an even-tempered way.

"This is just it, Samantha. You never want to listen to me. So many things are more important than me."

"I heard how you botched the talk with Robert. It's something to break it to him harshly like that."

"Hey. I tried my best." Pauline was about to hang up.

"Some favor," Samantha said.

Several weeks ago, Pauline talked to Cathy. Cathy relayed that her ex-husband was abusive from the beginning. She had always talked about his fiery temper even after years after the abuse ended. She had gone to a women's shelter and eventually, her ex left her alone. He kept his distance, at least. She had boundaries he didn't understand, of course, and a restraining order that would last the rest of her life.

"He, he called me, Samantha. Several weeks ago. He found out my name. He asked if I lived at the address I was at. I fell for it," Pauline said.

The thing was the ex's name was Mike. Mike, the same name on the sign at the lobster shack. The same name as the man who had pulled the gun on Monica.

"Look, Pauline. I have to go. I'm getting dinner ready. What do you want me to say? Call Cathy. Check in. This is serious." They hung up after bidding each other a goodbye with soft drawn-out words, wanting to hold on but knowing they couldn't. It would be the last call for a while.

Pauline turned and looked out the window, staring at the bright lights with bugs swarming around them, forever attracted to the brilliance. She thought about friendship, about love, and then she tapped her phone on her thigh before making one last call.

"Dear." She smiled big as a tear formed in her eyes.

"Why haven't you called me? Why has it been so long?"

"There was a surprise," Pauline said. "Well, I wanted to surprise you. A major surprise. I'm finally coming to visit."

"Oh, my gosh. You said in a month, but this is early," Cathy said.

"Yes. We're early. I mean, I brought a friend. Her name is Monica. We were on a trip with our daughters."

"Yes. I know that much."

"Right, right? Well, we took off for the open road. We were going to show up this Friday."

"Tomorrow. I'm ready. I don't want to go back." Pauline paused. "Except there's a wrinkle. We're close to you and there's a wrinkle. Did you say your ex's name is Mike?"

"Yes. His name is Mike. I think I mentioned that—" Her words bit closed. She gasped in an uneven breath. "Did he?"

"Cathy, I think…I think it was him."

"What happened? This man saw us in New York and then he appeared in Maine. We had dinner with him and this woman."

"Was her name Julie?"

"Fuck. Oh, excuse me."

"Nope. That's okay. It's just. They're thugs, you know that. I talked to my daughter about you. About you coming next month and she must've—He's tricky Pauline. He has information and knowledge of things. Can find people. It's me he's trying to hurt."

"Well, he tried to assault Monica, and she shot him. We are in a haze and unsure of whether to go to the police."

"Yes. Report it. Bring me up. His record will come up. He's done this—Oh god. I hate to say this, Pauline. He's done this before."

Monica got out of the car and paced. She must've heard the other end of both of the conversations. Monica must've known sitting in her quiet that she was a simple piece in this torrential slew of events. She must've wanted out. She was a victim and sourly so.

Pauline watched Monica pace around the light post as she hung up the phone. There would be no use in trying to calm Monica down. Pauline had taken her on this trip, and it was basically her fault that someone assaulted her, drawn into the drama of people she hardly knew.

Monica turned in circles around a light post until a police officer stared at her and she raised her hands, also shrugging her shoulders, also crying.

"Anything I can do?" He shouted. He mulled around a bit, looking back into his car for something. Rummaging and surfacing with some papers and looking back at her.

"Nah." Monica moved toward the car.

Monica opened the car door slowly and intentionally, as if she were under scrutiny. They could bring her in for questioning.

The officer continued to rummage, but it was as if he had eyes in the back of his head. Pauline could taste his breath. She rose with a jolt of panic each time he looked back at them.

In the spotlight of a high metal parking lot light with bugs buzzing around it twenty feet up, Pauline and Monica put on their seat belts. Pauline would take Monica to that diner after all. She turned the car on with just as much intentionality as Monica had. Even though the officer had gone on his way inside the station, and even though he could not see her anyway, she used slow movements, the same speed as Monica, to calm her and make her relax.

The car pulled slowly away from a place that should resolve the issue, should definitively say, "Monica has never lied in her life, and this is the truth." But that's not necessarily how the world works, how justice and law work. They were stuck running at the same time as someone else. In the same movement, but not the same guilt. The guilt, yes, the guilt was different.

CHAPTER 26

Monica adjusted into her seat, which was leather clad, expensive, the saddle leather kind. She held the piping at the edges between her fingers and turned to Pauline, pausing for a few seconds before saying quietly, "Gun it. We've got to get out of here. He'll lie. They'll think I lied, that he did nothing."

Pauline started up the car. They chugged along. Pauline was too scared to go too fast because she didn't want to get pulled over, but she scooted along as quickly as she could, as unseen as she could be in a red convertible. The top was down. Monica's sense of calmness and pause was over.

"Monica?"

It was late now, and the events of the night overwhelmed Pauline. It was all she could do but to drift off, so she tried to keep the conversation going.

"Yes. Pauline?"

"We're not the best of friends just yet. We're working on it, and we're getting close. All these events are driving us into each other. They bond us, in a way, wouldn't you say?"

"Yes. I think so. Pauline, you can really ask me anything. I've been wanting you to ask."

Pauline took a big gulp and thought hard on how to put the words. She opened her mouth, but there was a pause. And she looked over at Monica. "Monica. He…" She shook her head. "I know he…"

Pauline looked tenderly at Monica and put her hand on her knee. Pauline pulled it back as Monica flinched. So, she gripped her hands on the wheel and squeezed. This was her hug to Monica. This was the way she could show she cared.

"Pauline, there's been a lot of men in my life. I've seen them come and go. And there's verbal abuse and mental abuse and physical abuse. I've seen them all. But that man back there, just like my ex seven months ago, yes, physically assaulted me."

Pauline hadn't known abuse. She knew abandonment, that was for sure. But she had no clue about what Monica and Cathy had gone through, their lives behind closed doors, 'accidents,' and excuses.

"I hate to say it, but they'd believe us, right?"

"Well. They didn't believe it seven months ago and I could be a liar."

Pauline dropped her hands and thought hard on those words. Would there be a way out of this madness before it got worse, before the police really came after them? They were the ones that shot the gun. The mantra persisted.

"Would you take a test?"

"Yes. I'd take a test. Pauline, I've got scrapes and scratches, but I have to find out for sure they'll put him away. It's too much to see another one get away, another lie on my rap sheet pointing to me as the criminal."

When they crossed the New Hampshire border, they considered themselves safe in several ways. The distance felt secure, even if it was just simply that. Since Pauline was getting used to it and because they took cash and not always credit, Pauline stopped at the same motel they had stopped at on the way out. She was happy to lie back down on the stiff mattress, lumpy pad, or whatever she got. As long as she could breathe and take a moment to think things through. They had run from the scene of the crime. Were they criminals? Pauline just did not get it. She hadn't prepared for things like this, real life mishaps that could permanently alter your life's course. Pauline had driven the getaway car.

They camped out, each in their own rooms. Not needing to share, they both took separate spaces but met up in the morning as it was not past 3 a.m. to talk through the plans for the next steps. Whether they would turn themselves in, run, or act like nothing happened. They hadn't arrested them yet. The police couldn't have known.

Pauline was upset she was missing Cathy's visit. She didn't want to mess up a relationship that hadn't even really started. The one-year bond was strong, but it had only comprised talking. True, they exchanged I love yous and promises. They talked themselves through worst-case scenarios of a meetup, but the conversation never turned to a jealous ex ruining it all.

Pauline sat again on the floor at the foot of the bed and tried to find her center. Palms up, resting on her knees, she hummed quietly. She heard the ocean as it crested in and out at the beach just yesterday. She imagined from that moment the next moment, and then an entirely new scenario where they didn't meet up with Mike and Julie. They went for a tour of the pirate ship and looked in all the nooks and crannies. Her vivid daydream involved going to a burger shack and the both of them refusing a lobster roll. "Fries on the side," Monica would've said. She imagined them coming back to New Hampshire because they had forgotten Monica's suitcase. They returned to go home tomorrow.

For all the reimagining Pauline did, she could not recast the lie. She couldn't make up this story that was not true. Laying down on the same stiff bed, she pulled the unlaundered comforter up over her shoulders. She drifted into a nap.

When Pauline woke up, it was 11:00 a.m. She had missed the meetup and discussion with Monica. She pulled a sweater on and walked over to her room to see if the light was on and rapped on the window, hoping to see a face appear. When it did, there were two: Monica and Robert.

"What can I say, Samantha sent me." He chuckled.

"But Robert? How did you know we were here?" Pauline questioned the whole setup.

"I just. Well, I called your daughter—don't worry, she doesn't know a thing and got Monica's number. I called her and she was outside at the police station. She said you both needed some advice. I told her to go back to the New Hampshire motel and I would be there in the morning."

"I, I didn't mention it," Monica said. Monica combed her hair with her fingers and tilted her head back, now so perfectly calm.

"I realize this. Why?"

"I didn't want you to be offended. You wouldn't have allowed him to come up. I needed the advice. It's something I needed. I needed someone to talk to and, well, my friends wouldn't do this for me. They just wouldn't."

"Robert, let's go for a walk to the restaurant and get some takeout? How about it?"

"Yeah sure." Robert whispered to Monica, "She just wants to talk."

They both made their way to the restaurant, looking at each other with googly eyes. With wide and dim eyes, they read each other's expressions. They emitted a few grunts to guess who was saying what, or trying to provide for an impetus to talk.

"Well. Spill."

"Pauline, this really is all a mess. You've created a mess. I don't get how you do it sometimes." He coughed out a laugh.

"Monica and I really hit it off," Robert said. "Monica is such a great person."

"Are you having a rebound moment?"

"No. It's not like that. I mean, we just warmed up a bit to each other." Robert gasped in a big gulp of air. "We've just been talking and…We knocked on your door. Called your phone. You zonked out like a light." Robert raised himself up. "She's really great, and she definitely had cause to shoot this Mike character."

"Oh, great. What about me? I drove the getaway vehicle. We left the scene. What could we get charged with?"

"Nothing. It was assault. Plain and simple. You can defend yourself when someone attacks. You're allowed to run for your life."

"This guy Mike. He owns the one restaurant in town. Do you think the police will believe him over Monica?"

"I'm sure they won't. He has a record right—"

"True."

"He'll be in big trouble. You, Monica, must report this. I can take her. You need to get to Cathy before he does something rash."

"Right. Cathy. I still need to call—"

"Go. We'll take care of it. It's still been less than 24 hours."

Pauline drove off into the emptiness of the road, still as tired as when they got to the motel. One thing Pauline didn't like to do was drive alone. She wanted to share the wind in the hair, the casual conversation, and point at things and for others to see them at the same time. But this road she, the emptiness, was overpowering. She had seen it all once before: the recent growth of trees upon another growth of trees. This was not the place for sightseeing and sparse comments, and it was even more sour by herself. She lurched the car forward, only thinking about where she was going, what was next, her destination, and Cathy.

CHAPTER 27

Robert pulled the car into drive and headed back the way they had come, moving over large rolling hills, passing sparse cars, with a purpose. "Oh, Robert. This is too much. I really don't deserve—" Monica said. "You're like my superhero. I just don't know how to thank you. So selfless for someone you've barely met."

"I'll have none of it. You are a friend of Pauline's; you're mine as well."

The car was a recent model Subaru Outback. It had leather seats, which Monica thought was strange for such a rugged car. A moon roof capped the ceiling and Monica looked up and out through it.

"I can open that if you want some air?"

"You're such a gentleman," Monica said. "No, no. I think I've had quite enough air on the trip in Pauline's car. There was too much air at so many times."

"My moon roof is a little tamer then and open top, but as you wish. I understand."

That was all Monica wanted to hear. "I understand." That's all she had wanted to hear for ages.

"You should see me on a date. Boy, did I bring flowers and chocolates to Samantha. Every time I tell you. We'd go out. She'd get something. She only said she wished she just had the money to buy herself something. That I was controlling the money…controlling. Can you believe it? Oh, I don't mean to…I'm still hung up on Samantha," Robert said.

"Pauline filled me in a bit. I understand. I'm hung up on people too. Hung up on the way they are and the way I am without them. What I'm not without them. It's a tricky thing," Monica said. "You want to love people…I do. I really wanted to love someone, but I couldn't."

"I get it," Robert said.

"No one's ever bought me any of those things." Monica raised a simple smile.

"Well, let me get out my calendar." Robert pulled at his pocket. "This is difficult for you Monica, but I'll be the antithesis. Everything that guy wasn't. We'll get you checked out and report the incident. Then, we'll all be better, justice will be served. Whenever you think of him, just put my face over the top of it. I promise I am the upstanding man he'll never be. No one should ever treat a woman..." He muttered the last words to himself.

"This won't be the day I fall in love, damn it. I don't want to even have met you yet," Monica said. "I'll not have it. But you can call, and I'll consider meeting you for the first time on better terms."

They chatted for hours, exchanging pleasantries and more. They went through their worst and best relationships. Even though Monica commented you're not supposed to talk about exes on a first date, they indulged. It was better to really get to know someone and how not better to understand likes and dislikes than a little relationship history. They talked about first times and college romances. They exchanged their deepest loves that their exes had given them, acknowledging that they were exes and would never be in their lives again. "Some things still stay with you," Monica said. "Musty cologne, words whispered in ears on a good day, that first date."

"You really want to hear about my worst relationship?" Robert asked.

"Sure. Do tell," Monica said.

"With my son," Robert said. "My first true bold and blue loss."

"I'm so sorry. What happened?" Monica asked.

"Well, he disappeared. We weren't sure where he went to. Aww. He's gone now, anyway."

"Oh my, Robert. You must be devastated. Was he your only child?" Monica asked.

"Yes. It was a town scandal. I still live with it today, with the terrible memories, with people talking around town. The wife, err, ex-wife, said that's why she really left me because I hadn't been a man. Well, her words can bite. She probably…well, she probably meant it. Certain people never look at you in quite the same way. You never build back quite the same bond after a scandal happens, or something tragic at the very least."

When they stopped for a restroom break, Monica wouldn't get out of the car. "I've just had enough drama, and if one more thing happens, in a gas station, or a lobster shack or any of the places that have been on the trauma list this week, I'm just going to explode."

Robert said nothing and got out to fill the tank.

When he returned, he simply said, "Always buy a lady a snack if you stop for gas or otherwise. That's a gentlemen's rule." He held out granola bars, chips, a banana, a Coke, and a Sprite. "Uh. I don't quite know what you like yet." Robert pulled out as Monica tore into a granola bar.

"Thanks."

They cavorted down the road full of junk food and soda, giggling like teenagers as they carried on. "Which was the best road trip this week?"

"Aww, with you. You know it."

Robert stuck his head up, and a giant grin on his face grew bold.

"I really. I really enjoyed our time together, Monica. Under the conditions…I know…It all could be better. But I'd really like to see you."

"I don't think I can sanely consent but let me sleep on it. I'd love to hear more about your first dates…I mean chocolate and flowers for all consecutive dates, but what is the first date like?"

The station was a big white block with several jutting columns about eight feet wide. It looked more like a space station. Something so surreal, out of this world, was good for disassociation. It was neither a place for convicts nor reporting them. It was a mid-flight refueling station. That's all it was. Monica didn't want to be here, but she had arrived. Eyes rolled back into her head; she got out of the car.

Monica walked herself into the station despite Robert's multiple questions about her well-being and how much help she needed. Robert stayed in the car while she provided a statement and answered questions. Monica was a different person than she was when she let her ex-husband abuse her. She knew better now. She needed to turn in the god damn creep. He wouldn't do it again.

Monica looked back from the open door at Robert. Monica now understood how sweet Robert indeed acted, a catch. Such nice men exist, after all. It was just so strange he was so willing to help, so eager to supply support to someone he didn't know. Monica could only think about how utterly selfless it all was and how she never, ever met a man with this quality, a caring above himself.

When she looked back, she could see him bowing his head and scribbling some notes or reading a book. He obscured his face, but she knew he was there, and he would be when she returned. He wouldn't strand her, as far removed as it was from the way Robert presented himself. She had known men who would, who did. He would be in the same spot for a long while, she could tell, until she came back from giving her statements, and it comforted her. Strength to turn and enter.

Monica entered the station and went right up to the front desk. She freely announced the issue to the attendant, and they told her to wait for an officer to take her statements. "I've got a lawyer in the car," she said.

CHAPTER 28

Even though the top was up this time, Pauline was one with the open road, the possibilities that lie before her. Rolling over hills, she lost her stomach and found it again. She felt the sky on the horizon as it rose and cascaded above her a few hours later.

She never quite sorted all her muck out. She had always kept Cathy at bay, telling her it would be a minute more before she came to see her. "Apprehension was common," she thought, "justified, among late in life lesbians." Did she say lesbian? Did she at least think it? The word was so hard to get out. It filled her with her own self-doubt. Self-doubt that would no longer succumb to the passions that rose inside of her. She imagined the woman she saw on video chats, the pictures she had sent. She replayed the conversations, and the first "I love you" rang in her head.

Pauline adjusted her rearview mirror, looking at and batting away a stray eyelash before adjusting it back. Her suitcase still splayed over the back seat. It was askew as she had left in a hurry. She would adjust it when she got to Cathy's and make everything a little tidier. She rubbed a smudge off the mirror and only smeared it with the oils on her hand.

When she was nine, she had looked out her window at a woman who lived across the street. The woman's husband went to war, Vietnam. She saw him the day he left. The woman lifted her back leg and leaned in for a kiss. She left him. He left her. He never came back.

After he shipped out, as so many people did back then, Pauline watched after her. She felt it was her obligation in a way. Pauline's own father did not because he was too old or had some other ailment. A woman stopped by, well many women actually, but one in particular that caught Pauline's eye. She was butch. She had full coveralls when she came over. Quite different, Pauline often thought. How different than anyone she had ever seen. The woman always hugged her at the door.

From her bedroom window, Pauline could see the woman, see their intentions. One night, as they kissed, Pauline shut the curtains, scared, alone, knowing what it all meant, not only for the woman but for herself too. She hid the warmth she took in. In so many ways, she wanted to be and have the same as the woman across the street. She knew, and she buried the feelings as she closed the curtains that night. She never opened them, but her mom would come in and jerk them wide to let the sun in on Saturdays, always mumbling about her girl, who preferred the dark.

Pauline took to peeking through, only her eye appeared from a blanket of curtains. She thought they would never see her.

It was so dicey back then, so hard to combat the apprehensions of the larger world, especially for someone so young. So, she blocked it out. She blocked out the idea of women loving women for years to come. It would never quite be the same world it was after she saw those women from her bedroom window. But with the knowledge and a heightened sense of what others thought soon after, she pivoted her head to look away, to not stare, even today. Even sometimes with her daughter, she straightened her spine when they hugged, or Tera put her arm around Casey. She worried about the world, and that she knew these emotions in herself. Afraid of what her daughter would say, how she might look away or shudder, Pauline put most conversations about romance on pause.

The woman in the window, that she peaked through at, was inspiring and bold. She was edgy and lustrous. Pauline committed herself, shuddering or not, looking away or not, to finding her true fullness once the world had turned and she didn't have to worry about society. She made that silent promise that she would find herself, because she saw her plain clothed in front of herself, saw her face juxtaposed on this woman, found the same pleasure in that one view, and subsequent views that she knew she could never be different.

And here was the world, wide open and accepting. Her daughter was in a relationship, one that could lead to marriage. Here two lesbians with common bickering problems existed in a part of the world in the same way as everyone, every person, no matter what hue of the rainbow. Here she was, right alongside them.

Pauline touched her pale skin, washed over with a foundation that she had used for years. She didn't want the tear forming in the corner of her eyes to trail down her cheek. She would have to stop and fix it.

Pauline cursed her daughter because the tear was also partially for her. Her past and her daughter. Her daughter had grown into a selfish woman, and her nasty and privileged behavior marked her. She wouldn't do anything for Pauline if she asked. She didn't ask how Pauline was when they were on the phone or what she could do on this journey to save someone. It was a journey that was really to save Pauline.

A thousand thoughts rolled through her head, but one stuck out prominently. She must build her daughter back up again with someone she cared about. It might've been her fault, the divorce's fault, that she became messed up. Maybe Cathy could help her do that, build them up together again.

When they got lost in the woods, it was a first step to building back the relationship, building back their bond. It was a way Cathy had never seen her daughter vulnerable. Even if the woods scared her, she could see that things might get better. They both opened up.

When she pulled onto the street off the driveway, an entrance that might be to Cathy's house, she put both hands on the wheel. It could be the wrong address. She might be catfished. So many apprehensions pushed through her mind. The car glided onto the pavement, smooth and new. The perfectly lined wood shutters on the brick colonial characterized the house. Pauline had seen them in a picture Cathy sent of Cathy and her family, cobbled together, and found family, at

Christmas. The emerald shutters made the house so attractive.

She parked and breathed a heavy sigh, but didn't pause and meditate because she was here now. She was already calm. Her future would be bright. The confidence poured in Pauline's veins. Reaching over her seat, she adjusted the suitcase and centered it on the back seat. She patted down the lumps which were inevitable from a quickly packed bag. She would need to do laundry soon. Her heartbeat rose only in excitement as she exited the car and made her way to the front door.

CHAPTER 29

"Pauline." Monica gestured with her hands from across the street. "Come over here."

"Monica. What on earth? What are you doing here?"

"I said I couldn't let you go all by yourself. This is something we were doing together."

"What happened with the police? When they got there. Is everything safe?" Pauline asked.

"Yes. We had to drive back over the state line and then they documented my wounds." She stopped and covered her arms across her belly. She leaned back against the car door.

"I put Robert on a bus to go home. He gave me his car. This Subaru Outback. I never thought I could drive one of these, but I am. What is it with Robert? Why is he so…-so…just kind? Is he even a man?"

"Oh Robert, yes. Yes, he is so kind." Pauline eyed Monica, whose brow was now furrowed.

To Pauline, Monica seemed overwhelmed. She shouldn't have been there. She shouldn't have fallen into this whole affair. It was Pauline's fault. She told herself repeatedly. How could she have endangered the person who had become her best friend on such a cockamamie journey?

"Monica…I just…I'm sorry."

"It's not your fault. I'm here to get the bastard. Someone needs to be saved."

"How do you mean?" Pauline leaned back on the car next to Monica and turned to her with her question. "What could you possibly mean?" Pauline was nervous.

"Well, the police are going to arrest Mike. They said they would, but they said they're backed up. I knew what that meant. They've got better things to do. This isn't a priority." Monica's head dipped down. "I came to meet you. So, we could finish our journey. It's just. Well, I'm afraid that Mike might've come here. I'm just worried is all it's probably not true. It's just that when you accuse a man, a man who's an abuser. They lash out. You can never tell them they're wrong. That's how it always goes. I just…It's probably nothing, Pauline. I just want to make sure you're safe."

"Oh. It's fine. I'm sure Mike is mulling around his house; unaware they will arrest him in a few hours. How ever did you get here before me?"

"I got two speeding tickets. The Maine police almost took me in."

"Jesus Monica. Am I worth it?"

"You are worth everything, Pauline." Monica took her by the shoulders and then pulled her in.

"I am a woman true to my word and you've taken me on such a trek, such places. I never would live it down if I didn't finish the trip. Try to turn it around. Through all this, I do care for you. Have some fun for once. A bastard who takes advantage of women will not stop me. I won't let it."

"Oh, Monica, I'm so glad you're with me."

"I'm on this boat. We'll get through the weather."

Together they walked up the front steps, walking side by side to support each other. Pauline clutched Monica's hand and gave it a squeeze before ringing the bell. When the door opened and Cathy appeared before Pauline, she was like a lost treasure found at last. They embraced, and Cathy pulled Pauline into the air and into her house. Monica trailed behind.

"Oh my, and who is this?" Cathy asked.

"Just my number one support system. Just a woman's best friend who drove hours after a tragic incident to not leave her friend stranded without support. Only the best…"

They entered the house and removed their shoes. It was a cape cod but delicately designed. The walls had muted hues of green and off-white on off-white. The floors were slick, refinished original hardwood in all its glory. Not a speck of dust. Not a piece of furniture under a thousand dollars.

Cathy rushed to get some tea and crackers and set Monica

and Pauline up in the living room. Pauline introduced Monica as her absolutely best new friend and somehow Pauline could see that Cathy had got it. She understood.

When Cathy returned, she held a big tray with a kettle, an artist's creation, of boiling water, several tea canisters, some sugar, and a box of girl scout cookies. "It's all I could find to munch on. My kids are all grown. And sugar. Aww, it's the death of me."

They chatted about the trip, the voyage, really, out to Cathy's place, and all that had happened.

"Oh, my God. I can't believe this. It's, unfortunately, just like him. Mike is really not so good." She shook her head back and forth. "He can't stand that I'm gay. That I've been with women since we split up almost ten years ago. He'll never understand and he's so bitter. It's like a burden; a curse that plagues every relationship I've ever had since then. I swear he has my house bugged."

A creak in the floor made them all jump in anticipation.

Cathy placed a silver revolver on the table next to her. "He could come. That's all I'm going to say. You must be prepared."

"Surely that's unnecessary," Pauline said.

"Oh my. I'm so sorry Pauline. I didn't realize he'd start his antics again. It's just so hard for me to contemplate. To bring someone into this is so hard."

Pauline reached her hand out to Cathy to comfort her. "It's okay. I love you." A warm smile poured over Pauline's face.

"He broke into my house last week. He must've found our emails. I printed them out. I get it, it's childish—"

"I print mine out too." Pauline squeezed Cathy's hand as her eyes squinted and she flinched. And Pauline rubbed Cathy's back as the reality of what happened seeped in.

The more they talked about the incidents, the more Cathy shifted, almost uncomfortable in her own seat. "I'm just so sorry. I could never erase…"

"It's not your fault," Pauline said. Monica echoed the sentiment.

Pauline rose and went to the bathroom. It had been a long drive. She had not stopped, even though somehow Monica had arrived before her.

The herringbone towels were dark blue, and the custom soaps were Pauline's style. She sighed in immense relief upon seeing them. If anything, those few things in the powder room were symbols that Pauline would have a good relationship with Cathy. She hadn't known for sure, but now she knew after all their conversations. Their joyous laughter after each other's jokes converged on these new moments. These new first seconds and minutes they shared in person were so precious. Pauline was so relieved that it would all work out.

Despite the drama and the danger that they had come into on Cathy's account, it was satisfying to have defeated it all and to be in her presence. It was something she had wanted so much but could not escape her own reservations. She was now, she thought, totally free.

She dried her hands on the towels and refolded them, so they puffed up fresh. Where would they go now? Should she stay here as she told Cathy she would? The words they shared. When she said a long-distance relationship couldn't go on, that she would move and never return, did she mean it? Would she leave Tera and cease to cultivate the bond we built on this trip turned into adventure? This outpouring of life spilled all over everyone involved. She needed these people: Monica, Tera, Casey. Back home they would thrive, but here she was with Cathy, the one she had been so destined to be with, so fated to intertwine with.

The women chatted about the events. Monica spoke about how bad the interrogation was. They discussed the next steps, and Pauline was at a loss for how long she would stay, but she said to Monica that she wanted to give her a car, any car, her car. Pauline would get another one. The vehicle, a thing that embodied her ex-husband's spite, could not be remodeled into a liberation vehicle though she had tried so hard. "You must take it Monica. When we get home—" Pauline looked at Cathy and then back at Monica. "When I'm home, I'll sign it over to you at AAA. It will be yours."

"Oh, but I can't."

"Oh, but you must. You really must." Pauline was convincing. Her eyebrows rose high, and her eyes beaded on Monica.

Then they talked about their favorite movies and the boredom of being alone. This last sentiment hit Monica the hardest. She rose and said she would give Pauline and Cathy time together. She would go view the garden.

Pauline watched Cathy comb over a large, cultivated swath of yard. Monica strolled, bending to sniff all the flowers. In an open window Pauline could smell the pungent, green scents herself. The whole place smelled like magic. Cathy really must've put time into the garden. Time Monica probably didn't have. She had a job and obligations. That was her limit. Still, Monica strolled happily, reveling in someone else's labor.

Pauline leaned out the window and inhaled. She waved to Monica. "This place is marvelous."

Monica chirped back, "It truly is."

The grass was stiff but wholesome and Monica dropped, apparently relaxing, and basking in the sun. She looked so carefree, so easygoing. "With what they had both been through, with what it took to get here, how could it be any other way," Pauline thought to herself. The summer would bead on even the northern states soon. It was almost July.

Pauline planned scenarios in her head. How often would she have to visit? How long would it be until she moved in? Did she want to egg it on or push back? Pauline knew Cathy wanted more, faster than she ever had. But here she was with her support system, and everyone was having an enjoyable time. She wanted it to be true. She wanted the love and companionship.

CHAPTER 30

Pauline and Cathy were in the living room, chatting about the latest national news blip. Pauline relied on whatever Cathy said to be right. Cathy was right, in Pauline's opinion, most of the time. No one could convince her otherwise on this occasion, either. She hadn't seen the mass shooting that was making the nation talk over the last few days because she had been on a wild trip to see Cathy. She hadn't turned on a TV in over a week. Still, Cathy went on about the event and the national outrage to end gun violence. Pauline couldn't agree more despite not being filled in by popular media.

Monica lingered still in the garden, giving the ladies their time alone. Pauline often looked over her shoulder and guessed at what Monica occupied herself with. She stumbled out of sight but became the first thing on Pauline's mind. Perhaps she wanted to make sure she was safe.

They jumped at the sound of a cavorting engine on the pristine and quiet property, holding a simple but refined cape cod home. They lunged at the kitchen window to see a familiar blue sports car barreling into the driveway. Pauline knew from the start who it was. They hadn't told Cathy about Monica's events in the past 48 hours. They just hadn't spoken up because they didn't want to ruin the newness of the air, the blissfulness they had all fallen into.

Cathy pulled on the handle of a drawer of a small, engraved end table. A gun rested at the bottom, and she said, "I keep this for Mike."

Pauline glowered, "Mike?"

"Are you kidding me? I was married to the man. I put a gun beside me. He followed you from three states away. You can't be serious. I tried to warn you, but there is no way out now."

"Cathy. He's been following us. He assaulted Monica. I think he thought she was me."

Mike hammered on the front door.

"Damn it. He's never—"

"What are we going to do?" Pauline cried out.

"Call the police now. Go into the bedroom and call the police."

Pauline took out the phone and started dialing. "I am not leaving you." She was on the phone in seconds.

"We're calling the police, Mike!" Cathy shouted at the door from two rooms away.

"Don't matter where you're going," Mike said slightly less suavely than the way he came off to Monica and Pauline in southern Maine.

"9-1-1. What's your emergency?"

"534 Crescent Dr., Emeryville. There's a man who is trying to get into the house. He's violent."

"All right, ma'am, stay on the phone. We're calling the local police now."

"She has a restraining order on him. He's dangerous. You get it right."

"Just a moment, ma'am. Can you confirm the assailant?"

"God, just get someone here. I have to help."

"Ma'am, please stay on the—"

Pauline hung up and held her arm around Cathy, who was aiming a gun with two hands at the front door.

The knocking stopped.

Pauline lowered Cathy's arms slowly. "It'll be okay. Really it will. It's not that bad. The police are coming. Just calm down. I'll go lock all the doors."

Pauline locked the garage and side door before she remembered Monica was in the garden. "Oh, shit." The words issued forth from the finishing-school-tamed mouth.

Pauline watched Monica gathering fallen flowers and stealing a few from the bushes. She was making a bouquet. She leaned over and sniffed, inhaling deeply and absently. Her white linen skirt brushed the bushes as she worked. The wind carried part of the sleeve over her shoulder. Pauline paused for just a moment to sigh about how beautiful she was, and then she panicked. She must've heard the car screech in. It must not have registered. Didn't she hear them yelling? Didn't she sense the tension?

"Monica," Pauline let out suddenly, screaming into the thick glass pane of the sliding glass door.

Monica turned her dress caught on the same bush. Mike came at her hard and she could only flinch with a jerk and a duck. Monica sank to the ground.

Pauline screamed a high, even shriek, as he grabbed Monica by the neck, pulling his body left and then right and upward until she was on her feet, wrestling her left hand against an arm pulled tightly across her chest. She tried to break free. One hand gripped her right hand. And though the elbow bucked slightly in and out, the hand barely budged from the spot he held it.

When he saw them, Pauline and Cathy, a big grin stretched across his face. His tongue lapped out of his mouth and rubbed his upper lips.

Pauline's cheek flinched in disgust. Who was this man? Who was this vulgar disturbed man who was nothing like no one to associate with Cathy, the quiet, but passionate woman she came to be friends with. Cathy, who was tormented years ago. Cathy, who could not shake her tormentor.

Mike came to the sliding glass door with his arm around Monica's throat. He didn't have a gun, but a box cutter protruded from his right hand as his forearm choked against Monica's neck.

"I'll fucking cut her." His muffled voice sounded through the outside glass. He looked at Cathy with the gun now dropped at her side. "See what you made me do? You'll pay. You dyke."

Pauline locked the sliding glass door.

As Cathy raised the gun, Pauline tried to calm her, tried to tell her she might hit Monica, and that was not what she wanted to do. Still, Cathy beaded the butt of the gun at Mike's head, lowered it to his crotch, then back to his head.

"You fucking asshole. This will be your last step when I

get a clean shot," Cathy whispered. She took a second to wipe her face with her forearm and readjusted her aim.

"Cathy! You can't, you'll hit Monica. The bullet will ricochet off the glass. Who knows where it will go?"

"Open the sliding glass door." Cathy said the words slowly and determinable. "This man has been harassing me for years, almost a decade. He'll feel the sting of the pain on his crotch if I can do it."

"I'll cut her," Mike called out.

"Let her go Mike. This is between me and you. I'm showing you my guts now. Do you believe I have them? I can shoot you, something I should've done years ago. I should've shot you in your sleep." With the steadfast hand of a gunslinger, someone who went to a range regularly, she took aim with a wink of an eye. Cathy refined and patient, expensive taste and loving. Cathy.

Monica, in a full swing, shifted her hip, turned slightly to the side, and let her hand down like a gavel on Mike's genitalia. When he dropped his arm, she poked at his eyes with her fingers meeting at a point. Two hands at once.

Mike fell on his back and ducked his head in. Monica had punctured his eyes.

She lunged for the sliding glass door. Pauline popped it open and let her in, locking it again immediately. Cathy would not lower the gun.

"I took self-defense," Monica said, dusting off her pants. "Knew I'd need it someday. I just thought it would be with my husband, not someone else's."

"Oh. I'm so sorry," Cathy cried out as she unlocked the sliding glass door and came to Monica's side.

"I'd like to say no big deal, but this has become a thing."

"Cathy—"

"It's okay, Cathy. I know. I've lived this too. Some days, we need to put our big girl panties on."

Holding his eyes in his forearm, Mike staggered toward the glass door as the women backed away toward the living room and the front of the house. He whaled on the glass and moaned in pain. He didn't ask for help or because of the pain. The moans were only his anger not fully forming. His head pulled back and forth against the glass and smeared fluids of sweat and mucus streaked across Cathy's picture-perfect window into her backyard garden.

"I can never live here again," she muttered. Taking strides back, she adjusted the gun to her hip.

Pauline knew he hadn't the strength to get through the glass, to find his knife and stab at it or break it with the butt. The glass was too thick. The chair in the garden was something he could throw at the glass door. But he didn't. The kitchen window might break with a heavy impact. Pauline saw a baseball bat in the garage. Cathy probably kept it stowed there for him. It could eventually be her demise. He did none of these things, though they rang like alarms in Cathy's mind.

He barreled away, staggering knobby knee on knobby knee, still holding his eyes. And the women panicked. Where did he go? The women stumbled to look out the front window. They could not see on the side of the house where the garage was. All three came into a huddle.

"We must be vigilant and stick together. No one knows where he has gone. I will shoot him," Cathy said. "He's dangerous. Dangerous to the world." She raised the gun again and went to the kitchen window. She could see the blue sports car in the driveway. The door swung open.

When he appeared in the women's line of vision, they could see him hobbling down to it. He dragged his knee on the ground and swept his arm outstretched, looking for the door.

"What a wreck," Monica said. "That bastard will get years, I'm sure." She patted Cathy on the back. Cathy flinched. She still held the gun.

Mike pulled himself into the car seat and fiddled in his pockets for a key. He was going to drive.

"What a moron." Pauline looked away.

The three women stared on at him through the front

windshield as he started up the car. They didn't flinch until he took it out of the park. His head was down, and he forced it into gear with his shoulders. Raising his elbows, he looked like he was getting ready for something, bracing himself. Then it hit them. He barreled straight for the kitchen window, jetting the car forward in an instantaneous motion. It hit the wall, crumpling. The kitchen window glass shattered, flying everywhere. It was all the women could do to take two steps back before the impact. Cathy lost the gun. It fell to the floor, knocked out of sight.

Mike's body was a mangled mess thrown through the front windshield. He certainly wasn't wearing a seat belt. His body, cut and gouged on the windshield, protruded. His full top half leaned against the dashboard or out the window, touching the scrunched front end of the car, but not quite impacting the brick wall that stopped it. The wall, Cathy's wall, might have shifted a bit, but not much. The brick was stable.

"Is he dead?" Monica asked.

"Close, but I doubt it. Men like him never die," Cathy said. "They always at least haunt our dreams."

The three of them sat huddled by a teapot, an artistic creation, consoling each other. They insistently asked each other if they were okay. Cathy could do nothing but apologize to Monica. She was truly so sorry that it had all happened. She gushed and hugged her, and tears fell.

The police came barreling in minutes later. Cathy still had her gun beaded on a balled-up Mike. A few jerks and a moan emitted from his mouth. Monica had learned the moves and used them. She said it was something she was proud to do. Something she could only have hoped to do effectively.

"Ladies. This...We're so sorry, but we're going to need some statements."

A police officer in the background called for an ambulance.

A female police officer sat with Monica as another checked Mike for vitals.

Cathy explained the turmoil. The forsaken lover bitter about his wife dating someone new. He was always bitter. He was brutal toward her desires.

Pauline witnessed the whole of this and attested to the accuracy, verified the events. She fumbled over words about how she came to be here. The long-distance phone and Zoom relationship they started just over a year ago. She didn't quite know how to say that she left her daughter on vacation and took her daughter's girlfriend's mother on an adventure with her. The police scribbled notes and scratched their heads, but they didn't seem to judge. By Pauline's estimation, they had seen quite a bit. They had seen almost it all.

Monica attested that by Pauline hadn't kidnapped her, and that it was "expanding, a life experience, besides all the shenanigans." She continued to underscore she had no new trauma. She had a boatload of history she had been coping with for several years and just couldn't take on anything new.

When the ambulances came and sped off with Mike in the back, she told them how he went almost Scott free every time. Cathy noted the local police favored him in multiple towns, but she would fight every time to see him get jail time.

"It's always the man they side with," Monica said. "At least that's my experience."

"Not this time, Monica," Cathy said. "I've been coordinating with the local domestic abuse help agency for the past several months. Pauline, I've told you about it." She adjusted her belt and straightened her shirt, which was only slightly awry given the scuffle. "They're ready to help. They see the issues. The organization is getting stronger, and the police are responding. They've helped me before. I've helped them recently. And they'll help me again now."

"We're all safe tonight at least," Pauline said.

"They banged him up bad. I'm not sure if he'll walk again. He might not even live."

The police sped off, leaving the three of them alone, and the trio returned to the living room once again. Pauline's tea was still warm. They took in together for yet another solidarity hug, swore they would never forget this or each other. They each owed their lives to the others.

"I called the girls, Pauline," Monica said through sips from her mug. "They should be here by tomorrow. I called them from New Hampshire, the motel." Monica ducked her head and stared into the black tea.

"Wonderful. I really need the girls right now."

The three gathered their suitcases together and took them to their rooms. Each in their own space. It was the first time Pauline and Cathy met, after all. But in the middle of the night, around 1 a.m., Pauline rose and went to Cathy's room. Before she pulled back the covers, she asked if it was okay to get in. Cathy responded that, of course, she was welcome.

"You're welcome in my bed any day or night until I tell you that you're not. I love you."

"Cathy. I just want you, us, to be safe. I want to see that we are safe and thrive."

"I'm so sorry. So embarrassed to have done this to you. To Monica as well."

"It's not your fault, Cathy. It never will be. He got his own, and that's how it always ends up for the ones we call evil men."

Cathy pulled Pauline in and enveloped her arms around her shoulders, asking not to kiss, but to hold. "This is us. Do you like it?"

Pauline coyly smiled and said, "Yes, why, I do."

They embraced in warmth. Even though they didn't need blankets, they kept the weight as another form of security. It held them together. And they held strong for an hour or four until the sun rose and they knew they were still safe.

CHAPTER 31

"If you get it off your chest, you'll be able to move on, be better," Casey said. They left Pennsylvania, into New York, before one of them spoke. The silence might've sprouted a gray hair on each of their heads.

They were right back in the car together. This time they had a purpose, a destination. A real thing to do. What they must do. They must help their moms.

After a day of relaxation, Tera's mom had called her and told her about the incident. Shocked, Tera had nothing to say. She had never in a million years thought her mom could get herself into shenanigans, a predicament quite like this.

So, she called Casey and said her mom was involved too. She was, in fact, the one who the asshole had harmed. The trio kept the girls at bay because the three aging women didn't want to get them upset. Now Tera and Casey were upset.

Tera came back to her apartment from her mom's house and swiftly she took the bags from the front steps where Tera was waiting. Tera packed up the car with some snacks, a few Gatorades, and their light bags. The ones Tera got them both for Casey's birthday. They matched, but one was blue. Tera's was green. There wasn't much more they could do to make amends. They both still agreed that they needed to call it quits. Tera finally agreed she needed a time out to think about herself.

"Charades?" Casey asked. She ducked in the front door and grabbed a deck of cards to show Tera.

"I don't think I'll have the energy. Car charades are dangerous anyway. Remember?" Tera said.

They took off into the late sun, hoping to make it to Maine by the morning. One of them would sleep. The other, meanwhile, would drive. Switch.

They stopped in northern Massachusetts, near the border,

at an old mill. They quietly unwrapped the sandwiches Casey had packed. Tera opened a soda and corn chips. She must run it off. She dug in.

Casey took small bites and chewed with her mouth closed as if savoring the views of the industrial complex, abandoned, greasy, and full of metal.

"This is where I'm from, Tera," Casey said, biting into her peanut butter sandwich. "I'm from this industrial place."

"What do you mean?" Tera asked. "You're 'of' this place? You didn't grow up here."

"Simply that you don't know what it's like to be me," she said. "I grew up here. It's the same as every other place with hunks of metal, abandoned, torn apart. The people here, their parents, worked there. Their grandparents. And then there was nothing, and they moved away. Probably for the better. I moved away. I'm more successful than my mom."

"What place am I of?"

"You're of Cadillac, Audi, BMW. You're of that place and I simply work at the manufacturing facility."

"This is nonsense, Casey."

"It's true. We're not of the same ilk as your mom might say. I grew up across town. You've never been to my mom's house. You've never seen what her life is like. Probably how hard it was to fall in with your mom. How hard she tried to make friends. How she really needs friends," Casey said.

"Look. I'm sorry Casey."

"Your mom abducted my mom. She took her on a cocka-mamie trip and endangered her life. You bet I'm angry, Tera. You bet."

She had so much to say, and she had said nothing. Tera wanted to say nothing, but whispers of Casey's thoughts bit at her ears. In the morning, it would be over. They would go home with their own moms.

"It was a long time ago…" Tera said.

Casey was prying into the conversation they had on the way home from the Finger Lakes, the murder Tera had supposedly been involved with. She had no right at this point.

That's what Tera thought. She had no justifiable reason to know. What could she hold against her? She didn't owe Casey anything.

"It was a long time ago…" Tera said. She paused, not wanting to let on that she was over the entire relationship. She didn't want to have to lose Casey for good. When she said it, she didn't mean to hurt her. "What you mean, the man I dated? My bisexuality? You want to know about that?"

Casey stroked her hair. "I mean, if that's what there is to talk about. If it'll make you feel better, more at ease. You have so much pent up. So much hidden. I wouldn't be able to carry on a relationship like that. If you're looking to play the field, be wary. Know yourself before you get involved with someone else. Having honesty is so important. I learned that…yesterday."

"I loved him is all. And I compared that love to you. It was close, but you won. I wanted to put him to rest. I wanted to be okay with the memory of Mark. But with him, there was a secret. I'm sorry I shared that with you, but it did. It really felt good to get it off my chest," Tera said.

"See, doesn't it resonate when you come clean?" Casey took out a notebook and pulled a pen from the dash. She made two hash marks and put the book away.

"What are you doing? What is that?" Tera asked.

"I have a list. You want me back. That's the case, I'm sure. At least I hope I'm thinking about this the right way. Your tears waxed real yesterday at least," Casey said. "I made a list of things you need to do. When they are all crossed off, if they all get crossed off, I'll take you back."

"What, like a checklist?"

"Yeah. Like when I was eighteen, and I made a partner bucket list and listed all the things my partner would have. Well, you had them all, and it still wasn't right. So, now I have an amended list. You'll meet all these sub-qualifications or that's it. I'm really gone."

"Compliance and openness are on the list. Can you do better?"

"We never knew what happened to Mark. He might've pushed his best friend off a bridge. That's what the kids said at school. Those were the rumors that circled with certain parents. But I think he just escaped. He died inside, and he escaped to live a new life in New York City. That's what I thought." Tera thumbed her fingers and sucked on her lips. Blowing out a wad of air, she continued, "I know now that he really died inside either way, but I think…it might…he's not alive. He never realized he loved me back, I guess, and that's what hurt so much. I loved him for years after he was gone and looked out my window every night in the rain, hoping he was drumming for me."

"Oh. I get it now. I understand." Casey rubbed her shoulder.

"It's just that I've been thinking about the things I loved about him. The relationship we had is what I need. I need a man's lack of emotion—"

"Hey, what's the pleasure in lack of emotion?" Casey said.

Tera could tell she was offended. She took her bisexuality personally and she wouldn't have if it was any other woman.

"It's just there might be too much stress in our relationship. I sense it," Tera said. "It affects me. I might be more relaxed if I'm with a man. You never know. It might tear us apart. But it's something that I need. I need to find out if it is out there." Tera curled into the corner of the car and shut her eyes. Even if she pretended to sleep, she could end this conversation. She could waylay the inevitable a minute longer.

"I'm just going to try, Casey. I have to try to sleep. And if I find him and you don't wait for me, that's fine. You don't have to, but I always remember my loves. My two loves, and I might, if things happen, come back for you, and play guitar outside of your house and leave roses at your place of work. I might find the time to make a painting for you, spend hours reveling in the love I know we had. Because I know myself. I'm a passionate lover. One who you can never truly leave behind."

Tera shut her eyes to a speechless Casey. She wrenched her neck and forced her head into the edge of the plush seat of her Toyota Corolla. She ran her trimmed nails down the upholstery, waiting for someone to respond. No one did.

This fight wasn't over. This time out in the car would never resolve the issue. It was a resolution for another day. "Classic Tera," she thought to herself. She wasn't even able to talk out her emotions the right way. She couldn't even explain that this was why she loved Casey.

CHAPTER 32

When the girls arrived the next morning, they all went back to the living room. It had become a home base for the three women. Cathy brought out some more tea and crackers. They were still girls to Pauline. They were not yet adults with varied, inherited temperaments poised for self-destruction at any one moment.

"Dear, this is Cathy."

The two looked at each other headlong from distinct parts of the room. Neither could move forward, each frigid in their place.

Cathy still wore her morning robe, although a fully dressed Pauline was ready to go. She would eventually need some sleep, some peace to think.

Tera raised her hand and took giant steps toward Cathy. Her extended arm flopped up and down until it met Cathy's and then, taking her hand in both, her hands shook fiercely.

"Welcome. I'm so sorry. Sometimes you just don't ask your parents the right questions," Cathy said. She adjusted her robe belt to make sure she affixed it tightly.

"Sometimes parents want to have their own lives," Pauline said.

"I guess, dear, I apologized, foremost. This is humbling. I came to meet Cathy and yes, she has an unstable ex." Her hands waved back and forth in the air as her head bobbed side to side, emoting. "It's just I didn't get it. All this…is so. There's so much. It's been a stressful day, and I'm responsible for the worry I've created. That I've always created for you." Pauline sniffed in.

Tera cried.

"Dear, it wasn't you…" Pauline said.

"Mom. I didn't mean," Tera said. She came at her mom with full force and wrapped her long, gangly arms as far around her as she could.

"I didn't leave because of what you said. Dear, I'll always love you despite what you think."

"I'm so sorry, Mom. I just…Sometimes words are just…They just come out and I don't mean them. My thoughts of suicide are over, and they didn't come about because of you. You didn't have any bearing on what I felt."

"I could have." A tear lit up in the corner of her eyes. "Helped. Given you a unique way to look at things…to be."

"Nonsense, Mom." Tera's head was still in her chest.

Pauline pulled herself together and straightened her wrinkled shirt, hoping to create a more streamlined and appropriate appearance which was now beyond her control. Tears had run through her foundation. Sweat had picked at her eyeliner. She was over. Still, she excused herself to the bathroom to tidy up some more.

In the room, she found quiet. Pauline liked the quiet, the moments in her empty house since her ex-husband left and then when her daughter fled to college were divine. She thrived on doing what she wanted when she wanted, not being controlled by anyone. The ex used to buy her things as a show of power. He would buy her things and expect things in return. It only made her hate the new things: the jewelry, the car, and the vacation to Jamaica. She resented every minute. Now she used his money, in a way it was still his, to buy whatever was on her list on her terms. It was never a quid pro quo. She never owed him a dime or a kiss.

Pauline turned her hands over in the warm water, wanting to find one of those moments of quiet on her own terms. She would go back to her house. She would relish in the time alone a bit more. And that was okay. She didn't have to jump full pace into the relationship. She could still have both. "What if they took a week together here and a week there and saw how it panned out? There was more to a person than being always alone," she thought. In the same regard, she could never again hold on to someone so tightly. She needed space, and she realized that on the botched mother and daughter vacation. They left her without her own space, and she suffocated. No one could breathe.

When she returned, she was happy to see that Casey had entered the picture. She shrugged in Tera's general direction.

"We've moved back a step. Maybe we're not ready for a mom's vacation. Maybe I'm not ready."

Casey eyed Tera with affection. "We're happy going at a trot, not a gallop."

"Mom. I'm so happy for you and I hardly knew," Tera said, her arm around Casey.

"I knew with you from the very start," Pauline said.

"I guess things became just clouded. I can't believe you didn't tell me." Her face gave a big pout. "I'm so sorry we didn't get to talk about it."

"Well, part of the reason—the reason I didn't tell you—was because it's personal. You don't need to know all. It's my journey, really. But I am ready to share. I certainly am now."

"Cathy and I have chatted, and I won't be staying up here just now. We're going to spend a few weeks here and some time there and ease into it. The best policy, don't you think?"

"Absolutely," Casey and Tera chimed in unison.

"This has been such a fuss. Let's all go home on a long drive. Mother and daughter and mother and daughter. I'm not ready for Cathy to join us on this journey, but you will meet her. She can be the center of your life just as much as Casey will be a part of mine."

"This day. I think Cathy and I both realize." They looked at each other and Pauline nodded lovingly back at Cathy. "We need a break."

"Ha. I'll give you a few weeks." Cathy smiled and then frowned a pouty frown.

Cathy picked at the embroidery on her expensive living room couch. Her head rose to Tera. "I love your mom very much. We've been friends for over a year now. I just want you to know that I will take care of her. And I want to get to learn more about you. Who you are. Not just at Christmas. We might...dare I say...need to take a vacation together."

"Of course, Cathy. And I'm glad to meet you now, even under such terms," Tera said. "We'll talk and find out who each other is. I'm sure we will."

Cathy hugged Tera tightly. "I need this today." Then she pulled back and looked at Tera in a daze. "I'm so sorry that this had to be today."

Pauline joined the two in the center of the room, and all three embraced.

"Aww, isn't that sweet?" Casey said with a laugh. "So good together, those three."

Pauline, Cathy, and Tera let go and turned, muddling about, and getting ready to read. Tera lifted her bag. Pauline grabbed her purse and went to look for her suitcase. Cathy picked up the tray with the snacks and tea.

"Mom and daughter and mom and daughter?" Pauline said.

Monica nodded.

"Mom, that's all I ever wanted. More time with you. Time to talk it out: be us, be me, be relaxed and comfortable with ourselves. Stress free."

Pauline thanked Monica in private before they left. "Dear Monica," she said, holding Monica straight-armed on the shoulders. "I can't believe I drew you into this. What a new friend."

"Honestly, what are friends for?" She half turned her head and smiled, looking at her through the right side of her head. "But to give a girl the time of her life. Yes, some danger. But an adventure to remember for so many days to come." She tapped her foot. "Now I'm a little homely. You could say that. But this has been a week to remember. I will never forget it. It beats stopping off a ship in Saint Thomas any day. Nothing could be better."

"But Monica. It's okay." She clasped her hands in front of her waist. "I'm so sorry. I put you in danger. Don't you realize that?"

"Yes. Of course, but it was worth it," Monica said.

"You strange and irrational, unconventional woman,"

Pauline said.

"Unconventional… I'll take it. It's the new me."

"Monica," Pauline started. "Will you be my absolute best friend for now and for a long time? It's all I can do but to make things up to you."

"Pauline. It's fine, but yes. I'm looking for a new friend. A new man as well, but he can wait, I suppose. I'd love to go out for coffee next week."

"It's a date," Pauline said abruptly. She was happy to have claimed the friendship.

Pauline and Monica moved toward the car, Pauline carrying Monica's suitcase, as the girls chatted and said goodbye. Probably for now, but likely not for good.

Pauline opened the door of Casey's car and lifted her suitcase in. It was all she could do to not apologize more. Tell her how much she cared about their friendship, genuine and reckless at the same time.

Casey's car was more Monica's style. The red convertible had just not fit her quite right. Here she was getting into the car with her daughter, an older version. They had had rough and tumble lives that Tera and Pauline would never know. Danger and the unknown came with fresh stride. They were cautious and great loyal friends to those they cared about.

The team coasted away, Casey looking back at Tera. Monica's head was facing forward. Pauline couldn't blame her if she wanted to get going. She had been so gracious, so patient, so ready for anything Pauline offered the entire trip. Pauline would search her world for a way to say thank you because she still wanted things from Monica, her friendship.

Pauline and Tera ready themselves to be next. After Pauline embraced Cathy, pulling her head past her shoulders, and digging her arms in deep, readjusting them so the bond was tighter, she looked back at Tera. She seemed a little stunted, unaware of what could happen and what was unfolding in front of her eyes.

Pauline shivered at the thought of the conversation they had had way up on the mountain near the Finger Lakes. Tera had overpowered her, given her more pain than the simple sprained ankle. Tera pushed her to have guilt, and she had it. She was regretful and sorry and felt she could never make it up to her. There was no way, as a mother, she could not.

CHAPTER 33

As much as Pauline wanted the trip to be about bonding, she knew there were barriers, especially with all that had happened. She would have to pry at the lid. Not every mother-daughter relationship can be considered perfect. Certainly not hers and her daughter, but she must get some things out. As long as this drive would be, she and her kiddo stuck in the car together. Of course, Pauline had some check boxes.

The drive home would be long and uninterrupted by stops for gas and bathroom breaks. The two of them were afraid to converse and wanted to get home as soon as possible. Tera and Pauline must've sat in their seats relatively quietly for an hour before they sparked up some common chit chat that was only then dampened by lack of interest.

Some roads through Maine and New Hampshire were rolling and bumpy, without cars for miles. Everything grew lush. Fresh spring had dropped its bomb a few months ago and now things were fully flourishing. The leaves amid the pine grew with strength and purpose. The seas of green became trees with individual character up close. She could catch them each for a second before they blurred to the corner of the car window. She broke down each tree into its specific type, cataloging the ones with needles, the thick trunked, and the ones with sparse but bold and beautiful leaves all intermixed. The pines, usually clustered together in groves, would flourish through the winter. But those with unwavering trunks would last season upon season. The bold beautiful leaves gave the whole forest character. As much as they were all themselves, Pauline, Tera, Monica, and Casey, they had their own strengths. They carved pathways in the soil toward and away from each other.

It would scare Pauline to drive to Maine in the snow. She had a convertible. She didn't claim to be the best driver in the snow. An accident after her husband left, left her debilitated in bed with a broken hip and banged up shoulder. She swore she would never drive in the snow again.

Pauline tried to recover from what had happened. It's true that, like Samantha and Robert, sometimes things didn't pan out. Even if you tried a million times in a bland relationship as it was, nothing ever clicked the right way and partners ended up dissatisfied, sulking in their dissatisfaction, and things never improved.

For Pauline, the issue was this madness. Could this be the deal breaker that sent her gone for good? Someone hurt her, stalked her, because she knew Cathy, even just wanted to get to know her and be with her. Would it happen again? Could she expect it?

In Pauline's experience, her ex left abruptly with no plain reason except to be free and chase younger women. In this experience with Cathy, the fissure, the drama bomb, became less impactful. When he left, Pauline decided it wasn't worth pursuing, but she had hardly even met Cathy. Even though this horrible thing had happened, she could still love Cathy. It triumphed at the very least through the horrible episode, not even a day old. They left her to decide, and she already had, before it even happened, that she was in true love and nothing could break it, not even a supposition to chase younger women. For Cathy, she would intervene. She spilled out a laugh.

Pauline could only think that her daughter found herself in awe of what had happened. Shocked and frightened still. At least, frightened to talk. This was not the same as when her father left, either. The big event changed things, as she likely saw it. But the incident captured her. They did not define it as over. Pauline will never see Cathy again. Instead, Pauline had a choice. The decision lied with her. She was in charge of the matter and became left in control of the destiny. And somehow that made it better than her ex, where she had no choice. Pauline was in control.

Tera's wispy short brown hair mixed together, not messy,

but an electric style tamed wild with product. The product gave it control, wasn't it? Or would her hair be more tame, less energized, without the product? Homely, but more in natural control. That's more of how she would like to see her daughter, naturally relaxed, falling into the control that already existed in her life.

"Dear, how do you feel about all of this?"

"What Cathy? That guy? The stalking?" Tera asked. "I still don't understand exactly what happened. This was such a terrible incident, but it's not Cathy's fault. Don't hold it against her, really Mom."

And Pauline was relieved because it had been so much for her to come to terms with what happened. She had, in one way, endangered her daughter. It was her fault. Yet, her daughter entirely did not hold her accountable.

Tera immediately went to Casey. "Casey was just. She was my world, but I just knew it wouldn't work. I got out when I could, when it would hurt us both in the least. She will always be in my life, though. I will never let her out of my sight for too long."

"You will. I've seen it. She'll stray. You'll get jealous, and there'll be arguments that will lead to not speaking for days, weeks, likely." Pauline raised her eyebrows like Tera knew what she was saying.

"It's just that I really love her."

"Or you don't want to be like dad?"

"Yeah. I guess that too. I can't be a loser like dad, leave someone who still really cares. Drop off the face of the earth. It was just like death, wasn't it?"

Tera dropped her head and sniffed in. Tears formed, but she wouldn't show them.

"You know he hurt me. I never open up anymore to anyone. Afraid of abandonment. It's true. I don't need a psychiatrist to tell me that. I know."

"Oh, dearie," Pauline said. "I didn't abandon you."

"Yeah, but you did, sort of. Maybe it wasn't your fault, but when dad left, you left too in a way. You emotionally left. You were vacant, sad, depressed. Your attention wasn't on me anymore. I wasn't the center of everyone's world. I didn't have the parents. The figures I needed," Tera said.

"Dear, it had to be done." Pauline nodded, shaming herself.

"I know it's his fault." Tera paused. "But what he did to you was horrible. I just wanted it to be that way forever. However bad it was. I didn't want him gone. How much did you hate him? Why did he really leave?"

"Dearie, when you're together that long, it is best sometimes. I loved him, but if I stuck around, if he had come back or even called, and we got back together, can you imagine what that would be like? I guess I see that you and Casey aren't that far in, and it's fine to be friends, but be careful. You get trapped in codependence. I've seen it happen."

Top down, they careened through New Hampshire and over to Vermont, clicking their heels when they crossed the border. The Green Mountain state did not disappoint. Pauline could taste the crispness of the air. It gave her a chill as it rushed in the open windows and against her body.

Pauline never wanted to endanger her daughter. No mother would. But the root of her guilt went back farther than that day's events. Pauline never let Tera come out. She dismissed it and pushed her toward boys. Ironically, here she was finally exploring what it was like to be a lesbian and God, she loved it. She couldn't understand how she had barricaded her daughter into staying a child, staying straight, absent from her identity. She justified it that all mothers would do the same.

Her guilt would not dissipate. When she talked to Cathy about it, about her daughter and how she had been, how she tried to take her life, she told Pauline how she nurtured her own daughter and how her parents had nurtured her to be the person who she wanted to be. Cathy said there was still time to do this, to be supportive and caring, while still directing her to be a responsible and upstanding adult and citizen.

"Tera, darling, I want to understand. I'm out now. It was

a process. The day I came out to my daughter in person was the same day someone almost knifed and killed me." Pauline shrunk into the bucket seat. "I. The way you came out was also…I don't want to say it…dramatic." Pauline raised her chin to look at Tera from under her cheeks. "It's…that…you need to get it. I would've done it differently. Let you come out in your own time."

"Mom," Tera said. "If I was you and I had no one crawling up my back telling me to date boys again, I would've done much better." Tera laughed and then sighed. "That's morbid. The truth is. It hurts that you wanted your daughter to have a boyfriend, but it was my struggle that led me to. Well, you know what?" Tera looked past the trees out the window.

"Tera. I…" Pauline said. "Never again…I don't."

"It's not your fault, Mom. I'm positive about that. It's society or the world. Your own parents are just following along. But it happened and I am in recovery. I will be for the rest of my life." Tera rose, her chin mimicking her mom, and looked at her. "This only means that I can tease you unendingly about your crush and your newfound 'love.'" Tera said the last word in a sing-song way.

"Oh, please Tera, don't."

Tera wiggled her finger into her side.

"Oh. This is on now," Pauline said, pushing Tera's hand aside.

"Mom and Cathy sitting in a tree…K-I-S-S-I—"

Tera giggled, "Will you sit on the red seat together?"

"Will there be no rest?" Pauline blushed in the childishness of it all.

"Mom. I could make it much, much worse…"

When they stopped for slushies, it was a well-deserved rest. They had bonded on slushies since Tera dressed herself. After her first soccer game, they got a slushy, and it had never been otherwise since. As a child, whenever they left an event, they got the same drink. This day had been an event and Tera deserved a slushy. Everyone's mind turned to slushies when in disarray.

The Coke and cherry mix became Pauline's favorite while Tera preferred the off blue or lime green whatever soda. She fixated on the Baha Blast this time around. Even though the machine wouldn't freeze because of the summer weather and overuse, she persisted. Pushing the chill button to make it refreeze, she waited. When her patience was exhausted after about five minutes, she mixed some blue liquid in with the cherry.

The clerk looked at the two and smiled a sheepish grin. Pauline was a child. The washer coming out to her daughter. It was her being reborn, starting over as a new person. And she loved it. The least she could do was to include involving her daughter. She could give her the same chance she had had. Tera could influence her from the beginning, or almost the beginning, and determine who she would be as a gay, queer woman. There would be no end to the judgment of her missteps and confusion, her awkward moments, and endless questions. And she was okay with that because her daughter would be there to guide her. She relinquished herself to her daughter.

"Is it my turn to drive yet?" Tera asked.

"No, not yet," Pauline said as they walked toward the car. "I haven't had a gas station pizza in…ever."

"Oh, Mom it's bad. You will not like it," Tera said.

The thing came in a colored and designed cardboard box with some cellophane over the pizza so you could see it. The crinkle of the plastic and cardboard as Pauline picked it up made Tera flinch. "I know that sound. It's the sound of a lost, drunk college kid at 4:00 a.m. with the munchies. It means awful food."

After one bite, she dropped the slice and threw the box in the back. Turning to Tera, she said, "What'd you get?"

Tera handed her mom a sleeve of powdered donuts and Cheetos. "Road food Mom. It's the rules. When you're on a road trip, this is all you can eat." Tera had learned her lessons several years before. After trial and error. This college graduate could, after all, imbue a bit of wisdom to her mom.

"That's absolutely not what I've been eating, and I really have been on an epic road trip."

"It's never too late to start." Pauline popped a chocolate coated donut in her mouth.

"We could make it all the way to Florida."

They both looked at each other and said, "Nah…"

"Dear?" Pauline said.

"Yes," Tera said.

"Let's go back and get Cathy."

Tera paused and held her finger to her chin. "Ok, Mom. We'll double back for Cathy."

"She has a daughter your age," Pauline said with an abrupt laugh.

"Mom, I don't think…"

Tera and her mom shared silence and conversation on that long ride home. The words flowed evenly and easily as much as they stumbled to say "I love you" in not so many and so many more ways. It was a bonding trip, after all. That's what they set out to do with Monica and Casey. They had set out to make it all progress more smoothly in the future. But here they were Casey and Monica in Casey's beat up old car and Pauline and Tera alone working on themselves. They really needed to do the work. They needed to bond themselves before they brought themselves as a group to another pair. And they tried on that drive home, they did the work.

Pauline pulled the car out of park and turned the car one-hundred and eighty degrees before whipping her hands in the air and yelling, "Yeehaw!" Their hair flew wildly in the wind.

"Silence is golden," Tera yelled. They would take this next leg with a few words. The wind would be too strong. The rush and the roar of the breeze would drown out their voices.

Tera raised both her hands. The wind bucked them back and forth as she continued riding the rollercoaster with her mom in the driver's seat.

Pauline chanted, "No place like home." And they were on their way. Neither of them had ruby red slippers.

CHAPTER 34

A few weeks later, Tera affixed herself to the house. She had been going to work but otherwise moped around the house for several days. Cathy and her mom were erratic. They kept adjusting things: moving Tera's cup onto a coaster, fixing the blanket she put over herself to watch TV, and taking her dinner before she finished.

She slept in and that was the only quiet time the two really had. She strolled out of bed around 10:00 a.m. that Saturday, and Cathy tightened her robe around her waist. They were sleeping in the same room. Her presence was awkward, and she knew it. Her mother had insinuated the day before that she would pay for Tera to go to a hotel.

When Cathy left for her shower in the morning, Tera sat close to her mom on the couch. The manufacturer detailed it with pipping in just about every spot possible. She felt the velvety curve in her fingertips. Tera was back in the house living with them, too. Cathy, Pauline, and Tera, a fresh start for family. Tera and Casey might eventually work things out, but Tera had already retrieved a box of things from their apartment. Tera still had five checks to make. It was a tough list. She might not make the cut. Maybe she had to dye her hair blond or something. She didn't know.

"Mom, I just. Something's been bugging me recently. Something that I've needed to get off my chest. I've been thinking about Mark a lot," Tera said.

"Oh, that was a long time ago, dear. He was so young. You recovered, but we all understand it was hard on you. You went off to college and things got better, right? The last year of high school was tough. You always rejected all the therapy the school offered."

"Yeah. It's just. I'm responsible in a way. Like I did the crime."

"What crime, dear? There was no crime."

"He pushed Jason. He did. That's why he ran."

"Oh. dear. Oh, dear. It's not true." Pauline grabbed her daughter and hugged hard. "He was depressed. Jason left a suicide note. That's how they knew."

"But Mark. He could've planted it."

"Dear, your words are nonsensical. It didn't happen."

"Mark killed himself off the Tappan Zee Bridge two weeks later. We couldn't bear to tell you. Samantha and Robert wanted it to be quiet. You know how many rumors floated around. Well, everyone talks so much. The world's greatest couple could be found in mourning. They ought to have been."

"All those years, I kept my heart open thinking he was still out there. You never told me." Tera's fiery anger appeared.

"Oh, dear. It was for your own good. I'm a mother. It's because we cared. It's always good to keep hope alive. The whole thing was never your fault. That bottled up secret wasn't something to worry about at all. Aren't you relieved? I'm telling you now."

"It's as if I just lost my best friend."

"You did, dear, years ago. I think you knew he's always been gone."

"I always held hope. Always held myself ready to get right back to it. My partner in crime."

"I think you still have four weeks of grounding to serve for putting a bag of dog shit on your math teacher's porch," Pauline said.

"Served him right…Let's not talk about it," Tera said.

Tera left to go to the kitchen window and looked out. The fog had not yet lifted. Peeking up and over the ledge of the high window, Tera saw blotches of grass come into view and then become obscured. Tera went back to those days with her best friend. With her memories of what was good and the incident that was so, so bad.

Tera, at seventeen, had seen a dead body and not told anyone.

Tera wasn't sure why this recent recapture of her child-hood led her to question her sexuality, or now that she finally knew he had died, why she felt a tension of release. She felt freer than she ever had. And all she could gravitate to was Casey and how she left it. Had her insinuations that she would date a man been a threat? She wasn't sure she would ever know. All that she knew for sure was that no one could ever replace Mark and Mark was gone for good. If she found his doppelgänger, she now knew, she wouldn't be able to bring herself to not call him Mark, not fade into memo-ries of her careless childhood, before stealing candy bars could get you tough time, and shenanigans were a fire-able offense.

The creek that extended beyond Pauline's house that was just beyond the fog could have been that same place at the bottom of a bridge. It was just like it. But Tera was not inclined to go out and see it to revisit and that's how she knew she would never see Mark or his twin or stand in the presence of someone even remotely like him ever again. He was a monument in her course of life. Something she could not leave behind. Something she would share with Casey.

"Tera, see Robert. He will tell you. You can put it to rest."

Tera could think nothing more than of those days when she approached fifteen, sidled into sixteen, and wouldn't let go of seventeen. The trouble they got into. When she went to college, she pivoted, locked all those histories up and moved forward as a new person. She attended a school that none of her friends went to, no one from her whole high school class was there. She had locked up secrets, just as her mom had hidden away the truth about Mark. It could be she was punishing her; she just didn't know. Either way, they hadn't talked enough to talk it out of each other. "Did they really need to say more?" Maybe not.

Although those things haunted her, collected in her brain to process as she slept and emerged in everyday life, she could subdue her own reaction, the anger. Or, as it may be, resolve it through the truth by finding out what really happened to Mark. She felt she needed to share to build love around this truth, reshape her mind and the subliminal thoughts that plagued her with her anger. She was sure that Casey would help her through it. They could build happiness together, though it was not easily achieved. It was not always the white picket fence.

Cathy entered the room with makeup on and Tera snapped back to reality. She felt a little embarrassed that Cathy might've heard her get emotional.

"Hi dear. Well, we're all one happy family," Cathy said.

Tera could imagine they wanted some honeymoon time, but she was not quite ready to go back to Casey. She wanted to see if she had called her first. See if she wanted Tera. She couldn't push herself on the relationship for the rest of her life if Casey didn't want her.

"Look. I'll go. If you lived with dad for months before a divorce, and if you did it for us. I can circle back to our apartment."

Pauline came in and slid her arm around Cathy.

"Well. This is something." Tera leaned back with a coffee mug in her hand and took a big sip. "This is really something."

"Dear, Casey came by this morning. She left flowers. Here, I put them in this vase."

"What? Why didn't you tell me?"

"I thought you weren't over excited about all of this."

"Well. I mean. She brought flowers. That's. That's, well, something." Tera grabbed her keys and made for the door.

"I put the bag of clothes back in your car this morning."

"Thanks." Tera was out the door.

As she rounded the corner. She rubbed her temple, looking for the one living person she wanted to see. Casey would listen. She would want Tera to share. They would find this place together, at this time after childhood. Tera was certain they could work it out. "They would," she thought.

Casey nodded, a glare that sent Tera running. Had she not

gone, she wasn't sure if she would've found the gall to pine after her. This would be chance two and Tera couldn't imagine there would be anymore, didn't want to guess at the probability.

CHAPTER 35

The rain cascaded onto the top step of Robert's walk-up. It fell in waterfalls over the steps and pooled in a big puddle at the base of the steps. Tera looked down at it and paused. It eroded the concrete before her very eyes. Cracks in the binding pulled loose. It snaked into and overflowed out of the cracks, eating away the cement.

Tera made concerted, solid steps slowly up the entryway, hoping she didn't slip and flow down the street with the rest of the dirty water. It sloshed over her sneakers and seeped into her toes, but she persisted. She set out on a mission to engage change in her life.

The last time she popped over to this house here must've been when she begged to be seventeen, days before her birthday, picking up Mark for a night over at the local under-age club. They were bound to get into trouble. "A coffee shop." They had both said in unison when Robert asked where they were going. "To get coffee." Mark had chased all but implicating himself.

When Robert opened the door, Tera held the umbrella over her head and tears formed in her eyes before she spoke. "Hi. I'm sorry to have come unannounced. It's just…you ever have something really pick at your soul?"

She shifted her weight, and her shoes splashed some water in a shallow puddle. She moved to the mat, closer to Robert.

"I just want to apologize, Mr.…Robert. I need to say I'm sorry and I'm responsible one way or another for your son's death. We were erratic kids. I'm just about the opposite now. Do you believe me, that I'm sorry?" Tera asked.

Robert pulled the door back a little more and rested his elbow on the inside edge. His other hand braced him on the inside molding.

He didn't advance or retract. He didn't quite invite her in.

"Of course, Tera. I just wish it had been on better terms. I wish that all of us could've had so many more dinner nights together." Robert sighed. "That was a long time ago." He edged open the front door a little more and let Tera in. He ushered her in with his hand and placed a caring touch on her shoulder. Tera could tell he didn't really want to, and, after all these years, he was still upset about the whole affair, losing his only son. He had not so much tears but deeply welled dry eyes that might never cry.

"I'll tell you where he is but go with someone. It's so sad to go to a cemetery. But to go alone is so much worse." Robert moved into the hallway to get a paper and pen from a small desk. The drawer rattled open. He scratched down the plot number. "It's on Albert Street. You know where that is? Akron Cemetery. Here's his plot number. Are you going to take flowers?"

He held the pen and paper in his hand and waited for Tera to respond.

"I can if you'd like." Tera looked for his meaning.

"Oh, it's just…Yes. Just put them in the plot. I'll go later this month and clean up the remnants. Animals, birds, people sometimes get in and move stuff around, you see." Robert sighed. "It is so nice after all these years to say Mark's name to remember a bit of the history." He patted Tera on the shoulder, consoling her. "It was such a long time ago. We just wanted to bury it. We didn't want anyone to find out. It had become a total mystery to so many people. Well, some adults knew and if you'd asked…I thought Pauline had told you. Really, I'm sorry. If I had known."

"Robert, It's okay. It gave me something to look for to wait for and made me hold out until I found something better. It was what I needed to go on. I might've done things differently if I went about it again. I was so depressed that senior year and could barely get to class. It was so hard. It still is. For you too?"

"Yup. It will always be hard." Robert guided Tera toward the door. "We'll still go on. You can always come over. Give me some warning next time so I can make dinner." He put his hand to his mouth. "It sure is raining. You're going to get drenched with or without an umbrella."

Tera made her way back in her car, which was ready for a trade in. Next big service, she told herself. She didn't need her mom's money. She was on her own now and could handle her finances. Either way, it was embarrassing to ask for help, even though her mother could afford it. She might ask for a few thousand if it was expensive. "If her mom offered, maybe," she thought. Only then.

When Tera got to Casey's house, the sky had opened up. The sun was fading in the day, but there were still a few more wholesome hours until dark. A rainbow lit the sky. "Look. We were meant to be." Tera glowed.

"Oh, it's a double," Casey said.

"It truly is," Tera said, squinting toward the tops of houses.

"I want to take you somewhere. Really, can I tell you a story?"

"Well. I was just—fuck it. It's on the list. Tell a relatable story at least once a week. Where are we going?"

"Well, it sounds morbid, but it's the story of Mark and me. And we're going to see his grave. I need someone to say goodbye with, properly."

The ground was muddy, and after Tera tied her still wet shoes, she got mud on her hands, then her face.

Casey rubbed it off with her thumb as Tera gazed into her eyes.

"I really have seven stories, though I wish I could tell them to their full glory. I'll sparse them out over the next week. The joke had always been that Mark saved lives. That was his calling. It didn't stop with his first save at the lifeguard stand, age twelve. I'll have to tell you about that one from the beginning tomorrow. He swam so much. At least, until we were sixteen. Anyway." She changed the topic. "...After we went camping, though, the group went to the outfitters for a rafting trip. It's sometimes whitewater in the Poconos. It's really no joke."

She gulped air. "Oh, I'm no good at drawing out stories. He saved people. That's what he did at least once a year. He did this backflip off the raft. This huge yellow raft. It was yellow so if it capsized, which it could occasionally, the rangers could find survivors. This big raft. Eight of us…off on an adventure. Drunk seventeen-year-olds. We hit rapids, and it bucked, and this girl flew clean off. And he saved this girl caught in the water, spinning around and around. He dragged her out under his arm. He saved her life, but that wasn't it. That wasn't his best moment…" Tera took a breath and Casey was still listening. Hiking up beside her, she was holding Tera's hand, a slight gesture that felt so warm. She took in a breath of life and raised her smile more.

"Come on. It's just a little farther," Tera said. "It was all kid's stuff. We were bad, yes. We could've gone to jail. Maybe for a bit of juvi or something, but it was worth it. The times we sang in the car and careened down the highway, sipping on beers stolen from his mom's house. God, I wish you were there."

"I want to listen to those good times, Tera," Casey said. "There is so much more to tell me. So much more of our lives to share. There's so much time to share it."

"Hey, what else is on that list?"

"I can't tell you. But you've got two left."

"What's the time limit? How long do I have?"

"You've got." She tapped her watch with her finger. Then she looked up and into Tera's eyes. She held her chin stiffly. "As long as you need."

Tera held the flowers and then dropped them to her side. This moment. This sensation, as hard as she tried, wasn't something she could share with Casey verbally. She looked beyond her, from over her shoulder, knowing all she really needed to understand. Learning something that she couldn't learn any other way.

Tera looked back for a second and saw a sniffle and a tear emit from Casey. It doomed Tera to this place of sadness for as long as she stood there, and her feet were cement.

He was, in fact, somewhere. They had found him and returned him to this place. He never really wanted to be in this place. Tears filled the corners, then the insides of her eyes, and then it was a full stream. Her happy emotions of reminiscing only inhibited a darker, more shallow sadness.

In one fell swoop, she put the flowers in an empty vase and wiped her arm long across her eyes. There would be no new place for them to go. They wouldn't have adventures. They would never even see another dead body together. There would be no more cathartic moments. They wouldn't finally have sex.

Here was Casey. The love of her life. It was so much more to have her. To have stability and regularity. To not get into trouble knowing you'd be in trouble. They were adults, Casey and Tera. This was their life growing together, finding themselves whether they'd be together forever or not.

"I'm so glad you were honest with me," Casey said. "It's so hard to crack your shell sometimes. I love you, but to see past those deep-set eyes is everything." Casey leaned in and kissed Tera on her wet cheek.

"I just want to be open with you; to let my pent-up emotions flow out and have you catch me in your arms and have us be together. I can heal, but I need you. You're my lover. Be there for me." Tera closed her hand around Casey's.

Casey grinned. "We will work at it for the rest of our lives, but I'm willing. We can get through the tough times and then the good. Lay those tough times on me, Tera, and I'll see if I can handle them. I'm sure I can. Get them off your chest, give them to me and we'll be together through it. Then we can move on to a new world, our future, our glorious memories, our escapades with our moms on vacation. The daily drudgery of work. Whatever life brings."

Tera nodded as Casey, head bowed, and smiled at her full, wholehearted acceptance.

CHAPTER 36

The night's sharp light cast out unspeakable acts of day. It slowly dimmed, and the streetlights begged to be turned on. A bit of moonlight peaked from the horizon. Pauline pulled up in the convertible, top up. She still hadn't gotten rid of the thing. She couldn't bear to think about what it meant. The control of it all. It cast her as someone still indebted to her husband. She couldn't believe he didn't ask for a blow job when he gave it to her. A swift breeze made Pauline shiver it off. She relished in a car she could send off a cliff and not be any worse off for losing it.

Monica was waiting for her as she got to the door. Blue suit, classic on such a nice August night. "Hello m'lady. Don't you look simply fine?" Pauline raised her eyes from the ground to meet Monica's, which sat slightly above hers at actual height and not just because Monica wore a low heel.

"You look fine yourself, Ms. Pauline. Whatever have you done with yourself?" Monica threw her arm out over Pauline's shoulder and hugged in flirtation.

Monica held the door for Pauline, who shimmied in under the threshold. "Oh. This is just so magical. I'm so glad you could make it. It's going to be delicious. And there's no reason we can't cave to some gossip during it all," Monica said.

Robert greeted them at the host's desk. "You two. Marvelous." He put his fingers on his mouth and made a kissing sound. His delight radiated throughout the room. "You two were the first two to eat that cake." He grabbed Monica by the hand and stepped back to look at her glory and the expensive dress she had chosen for this night out. "Now, you can have it in the official restaurant. Your pallet helped make this…"

"Oh Robert. We like most food, but your food is astounding. Out of this world."

"I'll tell you. Nothing beats a quiet date in a small restaurant with a piece of cake to end the evening," Pauline said.

"Nothing certainly does," Monica said.

The staff dimmed the lights to low mood lighting, and they hadn't quite finished the painting in the back room, where Pauline and Monica had their first date, but the restaurant, Robert's restaurant, was open. Monica dug the toes of her shoes into the treated cement floor. Filled with spirals and spirals, loose geometry, the pattern memorized. "This floor must've cost a fortune." She hummed lightly as she put her napkin, a thick cloth embroidered with cross stitching, in her lap.

They ordered with small card stock menus; the kind that are changed out often as the menu changes. A faux gold frame held the paper in place and gave it structure to hold on to. "Steak tartare," Pauline said.

"Oh, that's what I—"

"You should, Monica."

"The fish though…"

"Another time. He'll make it for you at home. If your mouth is watering for the steak, get the steak."

The food came out, but not Robert. "Oh, he must be busy," Pauline said. "This is his big night, too." They sat in delight, tasting morsel after morsel and comparing it to the previous with moans and hums.

As the night wore on, Monica became more anxious, excited as a schoolchild ready to see her date at the dance. When Robert appeared, he was greasy but, as always, full of life.

Robert came out, wiping his hands on the towel hanging from his apron. "Well, what do you think?" He rubbed his nose on his shoulder.

"Perfect." Monica cooed. "Why don't you sit with us?"

"Oh, I can't. But really, what's your take?"

Their tongues watered at the very tip even as they smelled the plate coming out. It was the kind of food that made you satisfied from your toes to the tips of your fingers. The body relaxed with digestion and eyes sunk weary with delight.

"It's really superb." Monica bobbed her head rapidly.

"Delightful chivalry for the mouth," Pauline said.

"You always had the quotable take, Pauline."

Monica put her fork down while Pauline finished the last bite.

"Robert, you've really outdone yourself this time." Pauline stiffened up her spine to attention. Robert was no longer hers. He was no longer her best friend. But Monica hadn't slid totally into his life. They were still reasoning things out, seeing if they would get along. Monica dished every chance she had with Pauline, but all truth told Pauline didn't want to hear it because it hurt to loan such a good friend out. He was much less available.

When she heard, Samantha bailed over with squinting eyes and, well, jealous. She had nothing nice to say, but that's the way it went with Samantha. She was off on her own selfish planet. Pauline felt fine thinking that because she genuinely loved Samantha. Just as much as Robert. She still strived to spend time equally. Monica was an excuse to be with Robert and have Samantha not rage on her. She sort of understood, somehow.

"Well. Next is the cake. The grand finale. I hope you like it."

"Was wonderful the first time around," Pauline said.

"I'm just sorry I couldn't make it to four courses. We're just not set up for it yet. I wouldn't recommend the Brussels sprouts, regardless. It's not my dish." Robert rubbed the front of his nails on his chest and gave a flat smile.

"Pauline, dear. You are coming to the food party Max is throwing? Right."

"Oh, Max and Linda, right?"

"Yes. I'll be cooking. Monica might need a date? It's the nineteenth. Please say you can make it for the both of us. Monica and I." Robert pulled his arm around Monica tenderly and gave her a squeeze.

Monica raised her hand to touch his forearm with affection.

"I'd love to, but I'll have to check my calendar tomorrow.

Let me get back to you, Monica." Pauline nodded first at Monica and then at Robert with finality. They decided. She would attend either way.

When the stars started popping into an increasingly dimly lit sky, Pauline scurried out the front door, leaving Monica embracing Robert. They were surely going home together. She had done that. She had brought people together that genuinely liked each other, got along perfectly. Suavely, she ran her hand through a weary, exhausted hair, done up that morning, sighing that she had really done something good.

"We didn't even talk about the girls." Monica had exclaimed when Pauline had sat up to leave and grabbed her purse to get a tip for the server.

"Who needs them?" Pauline laughed. "They've been in our lives long enough. It's only ever nice to get away from them now. They're adults and don't need us prying. They make it through, I'm sure." Pauline pulled head back and looked up at Monica just before she moved to go to Robert. "The kids are fine. We're fine. That's all we need to know."

She shuffled to the car to avoid some puddles. The inside of the restaurant had been so nice, almost a universe of decadence and pomp. The decorations were bold and glittering, and they presented the ravishing food exquisitely. Now, she was out again in the world. Solo again, and she stepped lightly to avoid cracks and missteps into the muck.

A pleasant sigh escaped from Pauline, and she shrugged with her hands at the wheel. She tilted her head to look back at the window, half caught in the restaurant's shadow. She had really lucked out when she parked because cars packed every spot up and down the block.

When she looked up, Monica had settled in at the window, making sure Pauline got the car started and leaped off to her next destination all right. She gave a little wave in the window and Pauline looked back and raised her hand. Pauline paused again and waited with no intention of rushing. She looked back and Robert leaned over her from behind. He, too, looked out and waved into the night.

She had no plans that night but made her way home for an evening alone and some silence. She cherished the time to reflect but would be busy about the house getting ready for her particularly important guest. Dusting would need to be done, and she would need to make sure the dishes were done. Pauline would prepare with her last ounce of energy for her partner.

Cathy would arrive with delectable sweets and practical gifts, and they would go out tomorrow. Most nights they were together, but Monica had planned this night for her and Pauline to check in. That's what Pauline loved about it all now. Cathy and Pauline linked loosely, separate but together. Perhaps they bound the stronger for it. They spent time and when Pauline needed a breath in the dark, to just be and feel her soul, she'd go home. It was that simple. The two-day drive was nothing for love. And what kept them together was the freedom and candidness about space.

THE END

Acknowledgements

You know who you are. And damned if I'd be here without you.

About the Author

"S.E. Smyth is writing away as much as she can. She is inspired by history and stories that have not been told, pulling words from true events, her lived experience, and education in history.

S.E. has published two novels with NineStar Press, Hope for Spring (2023), and Criminal by Proxy (2022). In The Woods (2023) and The NeverSleep (2025) were released by Spectrum Books. S.E. writes the stories that are hard to tell. Her accounts are never exactly how they happened, and she firmly believes it is reparative to reimagine.

Excellent LGBTQ+ fiction by unique,
wonderful authors.

Thrillers
Mystery
Romance
Literary
Young Adult
& More

Visit us at
www.spectrum-books.com

Or find us on Instagram
www.instagram.com/spectrumbookpublisher

www.ingramcontent.com/pod-product-compliance
Lightning Source LLC
Chambersburg PA
CBHW010342170726
48283CB00009B/2919